Hawley Smart

Without love or licence

A tale of South Devon

Hawley Smart

Without love or licence
A tale of South Devon

ISBN/EAN: 9783744739023

Printed in Europe, USA, Canada, Australia, Japan

Cover: Foto ©Andreas Hilbeck / pixelio.de

More available books at **www.hansebooks.com**

WITHOUT LOVE OR LICENCE

A Tale of South Devon

BY

HAWLEY SMART

AUTHOR OF 'BREEZIE LANGTON' 'THE MASTER OF RATHKELLY'
'LONG ODDS' ETC.

IN THREE VOLUMES

VOL. I.

London

CHATTO & WINDUS, PICCADILLY

1890

PRINTED BY

SPOTTISWOODE AND CO., NEW-STREET SQUARE

LONDON

CONTENTS

OF

THE FIRST VOLUME

WITHOUT LOVE OR LICENCE

CHAPTER I

THE DRAGON INN

WHAT induced Joe Mercer to take the old Dragon Inn was a thing that puzzled his friends and acquaintances not a little. Those who knew him best deemed him the last man to throw his money away in foolish speculation, and yet what could have induced him to take a dilapidated roadside inn, from which the custom had departed the last ten years, or more? Joe Mercer had come to Exmouth about thirty years before the commencement of this history. He had no apparent command of money to start with, still whatever business he took in hand throve, and for all his pleasant, good-humoured, somewhat unctuous manner there were very few who could lay claim to having got the best of Joe Mercer at a bargain, though there were plenty who could tell a different tale. Shortly after his arrival at Exmouth, he married a woman a little older than himself, a bold black-browed virago, who, though attractive, both in appearance, and from the possession of a little bit of money, had failed to find a man hardy enough to face the brunt of her vixenish tongue for a lifetime. The command of a little more capital enabled Mercer to further extend his operations, and whatever he turned his hand to—and he was a regular Jack-of-all-trades—Joe Mercer made money at. He had dabbled in pretty nearly everything, but whether it was coal or corn, timber or turnips, he always came out of the speculation some- what the better for it. He was by this time reputed a ' warm man ' amongst his friends, but neither he nor his wife was much addicted to show. They lived quietly, and though no one doubted Joe Mercer had money, nobody suspected him of being rich.

Still, what could have made him take the old Dragon Inn? A house with a history, certainly, but a house, one would think, of which the history was ended; while, as every one knew, it had been shut up altogether for the last five years. Standing about a mile out of the town, a little off a road, which, running through a rich farming country, led to a large fishing village only, it was not likely to attract much custom. Years ago, when the Dragon was a prosperous house, it was much the fashion amongst the visitors and people of Exmouth to have jaunts and junketings there in the summer-time. Picnics were held there. The big room at the Dragon was just the thing for a dance. It was a pleasant stroll from the town, and it was the fashion to declare that there were no such strawberries and cream anywhere as were to be had at the Dragon. The hostess had some renown as a cook, and it was considered amongst the young bloods who frequented the neighbouring town, quite the correct thing to dine there occasionally. But after dark, and more especially during the autumn and winter nights, rumour declared that the Dragon entertained very different guests, that instead of modish young gentlemen in top-boots and buckskins and caped riding-coats, it was crowded with black bearded men in semi-nautical attire, and whose speech

was garnished with a profusion of those ex-
pletives so much in vogue about the time that
Nelson swept the seas. Report said that the
horses of the Dragon did a deal more work by
night than ever they did on the farm attached
to the Inn by day, and that the granaries contained more ankers of brandy than sacks of
corn.

But all this was a thing of the past. Free
trade had pretty well killed smuggling, and
so far reduced the profits as to make the game
no longer worth the candle. With railways,
too, came the facility of travel, and the Exmouth merrymakers went further afield for
their revelry. Still it was, no doubt, mainly
the decline of smuggling that produced the
decline of the Dragon. The old house
struggled bravely along for some time under
tenant after tenant, these latter mostly

endeavouring to get their living out of the land attached to it rather than by the inn itself; indeed, the last landlord of the Dragon had finally decided to shut up the house as an inn, and confine himself solely to farming till his lease should be up.

'It's odd, very odd,' said one of Joe Mercer's intimates; 'it bangs one altogether. Old Joe and his wife are a managing pair, but they have no experience in the liquor trade. He can't expect to get a living out of that old tumbledown house, and if Crank couldn't make the farm pay, it ain't likely that he can. He has done one or two smart specs in corn, no doubt, but that don't teach a man how to grow it, and Joe is over old to learn.' However, the new tenant of the Dragon, in spite of a good-humoured and slightly jocular manner, was an adept at keeping his mouth closed.

He would talk freely with any one upon any subject, and was apparently as open and candid a man as you would wish to meet; but for all that, you never got a word out of him about his own concerns. And though his neighbours were full of inquiry as to what had induced him to take the place, they got no scrap of information from Joe Mercer. He put them off with all sorts of jesting replies. 'It was a nice cheap place; he wanted country air. He was getting too old for business. A bit of a farm like that would just serve to amuse him.'

' "Old," Joe?' retorted one of his cronies, 'gammon! you ain't very far past fifty, and you're tough as pin wire. Why, it'll cost you a mint of money to put the old tumble down place in repair.' To which Mr. Mercer merely replied, that 'he supposed he should have to wear a bit of money over it.'

It soon became evident that whatever his motive might be in taking the Dragon, he had no intention of spending money over the house. A bar and bar-parlour were speedily fitted up, with little regard to ornamentation; a licence to sell wine, beer, and spirits taken out, and that apparently was as much as Joe Mercer thought necessary to do for the public. He furnished as many rooms in the rambling old building as his family required, and indeed, in respect to bedrooms, seemed to have gone to rather unnecessary expense, having two or three to spare; the old signboard was renovated till the victim of St. George shone resplendent in many colours, and then he briefly announced his appearance in the 'public line' in the local papers, and sat himself down to wait for customers.

He had certainly not gone to much expense, being even in that matter of the signboard careful of his outlay; but still, it seemed, his friends were like to prove true prophets, and that in all probability he would never see his money again. The Dragon had now been re-opened some months, and Joe Mercer, to all appearance, was still waiting for customers who seldom came. The few pints of beer and the odd glasses of brandy-and-water that he sold would surely never pay either his rent or his licence; while as for the land, Mr. Mercer seemed to trouble his head very little about that, and certainly no one would be likely to accuse him of high farming. However, to the astonishment of his friends, the landlord of the Dragon seemed quite contented with the present state of things. He declared that business was on the increase, despite there being no visible signs of such being the case; said that to re-establish an inn that had been given up for some years was a slow process, and that it would ' pay right enough in the long run.' Meanwhile the only noticeable thing was that of the few customers who did frequent the Dragon, most of them were strangers to the neighbourhood.

Joe Mercer was blessed with only two children; of these Sam, the elder, had some years since left the paternal nest, and, with his father's assistance, started in business on his own account. When his intimates inquired of Joe what his son was doing, that worthy would reply briefly, with an expressive wink, ' horses;' but Mrs. Mercer, who was more communicative, always proudly described Sam as ' a gentleman

on the turf.' Whatever Sam Mercer's exact
position might be, when he periodically made
his appearance he was always dressed in good
clothes, and had apparently plenty of money
in his pockets. As for Sarah, more familiarly
known as Sally Mercer, she was a good-looking,
black-browed wench, who had inherited a good
bit of her mother's energetic disposition and
passionate temper. For the rest she was a vain,
ambitious, pleasure-loving young woman, who
had already made herself rather notorious by
the lengths to which she had carried her some
what numerous flirtations; but, with all this,
the girl never lost sight of the one great
object of her ambition, and in this she was
constantly encouraged by her father. Miss
Mercer was not satisfied with the companion-
ship of the tradespeople, farmers, cornfactors,
&c., amongst whom her lot was cast. She

aspired to ascend in the social scale, and knew that the one way she could achieve this was by marriage.

'Don't you throw yourself away, Sal,' her father would say; 'you're a good-looking lass, and won't go to your husband empty-handed. Only marry a gentleman, and I'll see you've brass enough to ruffle it with the best of 'em; remember, they are just as much caught by a pretty face as a shopman, and you're better-looking than ever your mother was, and she was a clipper in her day.'

Miss Mercer, upon the whole, approved of the move from Exmouth to the Dragon. It was a much more roomy house than the one they had vacated, and it was no distance from her numerous friends; indeed, as she remarked to herself, it was a very nice distance for her admirer of the evening to see her home. At first she had some thoughts of occasionally officiating in the bar, but after two or three days' experience of the few customers who looked in, she made up her mind, unless more attractive metal turned up, to leave that domain entirely to her mother, and the 'young lady' officially engaged for the post.

This latter damsel had always been hopelessly puzzled by a peculiar clause in her agreement, to wit, a stipulation that she should return to her own home in Exmouth to sleep. Why Mr. Mercer could not find her a bedroom in a house with so much spare room as the Dragon passed her comprehension. The men employed on the farm lived over the stables, and the two country girls who acted as handmaids to Mrs. Mercer slept in a cottage hard by, so that virtually after nine o'clock, except perhaps for a chance traveller, there was nobody in the inn save the family themselves. These arrangements were peculiar, no doubt, but not more so than Joe Mercer's taking the Dragon at all.

'He's a long-headed 'un, is Joe,' remarked one of his intimates, ' but he'll muddle all his money away over that there Dragon, mind me if he don't.'

We can most of us reckon among our acquaintances some few whom we rather dread coming across, and his friends, as a rule, dreaded meeting Mr. Tootell. Always a gossip and a busybody, since retiring from business that gentleman had dedicated his leisure to assiduous inquiry into the affairs of his neighbours, and the taking of the Dragon Inn by Joe Mercer was a thing that at once

attracted his attention. Mr. Tootell having
made his own money in the ' public line,' and
having an infinite belief in his own wisdom,
considered that no man could know better
than himself as to what promised to be a
paying property in that way. It was only
friendly to give Joe a hint of how things
ought to be done. Of course, he was
innocent as a baby about the liquor traffic,
and Mr. Tootell resolved to initiate him into
a few of the tricks of the trade. Then Mr.
Tootell discovered that to walk out to the
Dragon, see how Joe was getting on, and re-
fresh himself, with a glass of amber-coloured
ale, was a very pleasant way of passing the
forenoon, until at last the host of that inn
began to weary exceedingly of his visitor.
Mr. Tootell understood the business too well
not to speedily see that the Dragon gave no

signs of ever becoming a paying concern, and it seemed a most extraordinary thing to him that shrewd old Joe Mercer did not see it also ; he must be losing money over it, it might be slowly, but it must be surely ; and the thing that surprised Mr. Tootell was that he seemed quite indifferent about it. Now, the losing of money in anything was a thing about which Joe Mercer had never been known to be phlegmatic ; on the contrary, ' Cautious Joe,' as his intimates sometimes dubbed him, was well known to be exces-sively chary of scorching his fingers ; his withdrawal from a concern that did not promise to pay fairly might be confidently predicted ; the one mistake that he had never been known to fall into was that of throwing good money after bad. A favourite aphorism of his was ' the first loss is the best and cheapest.' What on earth made him take the Dragon Inn to begin with? What on earth made him go on with it, was a problem which so interested Mr. Tootell that he devoted himself to its solution with much energy. Like most men of the Paul Pry type he was pachydermatous. Mrs. Mercer was downright rude to him, her daughter flouted him, as, indeed, she always had done, while, thick-skinned as Mr. Tootell indubitably was, even he could not regard Joe's welcome as cordial—still he continued his visits with undiminished pertinacity, and eventually, like other bores, he got to be endured; he was a cross that had to be borne, and, as Joe Mercer said slyly, what his wife's tongue failed to bring about, it was hopeless for any one else to attempt.

'Excellent ale this, Joe,' quoth Mr.

Tootell, as he sat in the bar, in the full
enjoyment of a pipe and a cool tankard.
'Reyther too strong to give to customers,
though; might get into their heads, and we
don't want 'em drunk on the premises, do
we? Wants a little judicious blending, eh,
Joe?'

'I only keep the one sort of ale,' replied Mercer, 'we've not enough custom for
varieties.'

'Pooh. What's that got to do with it?
The first duty of an innkeeper is to take care
of his customers' health and his own pockets,
which means take care they never get their
liquor too strong. By the way, who was
that fellow I saw in here yesterday afternoon?'

'Don't know,' replied Joe. 'He is a
stranger in these parts, I fancy.

'Odd, uncommon odd. I thought you looked as if you had met before.'

'So we have,' replied Mercer. 'He has been in here two or three times for refreshment of some sort.'

'Curious, very curious; not the first stranger by two or three that I've met at your place, Joe. Now, what can bring strangers in these parts to the Dragon? Your ale is good, I grant, but it ain't such tip-top tipple as all that. Besides, the place hasn't a name, you know.'

'Never you mind, Tootell; the Dragon had a good name in days gone by, and will have again, you'll see. It don't follow because you've given up business that every one else is to do the same.'

'Don't be edgy, Joe. I take a friendly interest in you. A business like this is depressing, and makes a man irritable, 1 know. I bear you no malice. Cheer up, Joe. I wish you luck, and bid you good afternoon.'

As Mr. Tootell left the house he encountered the stranger who had attracted his attention on the previous day, and marvelled much what this constant customer, as he termed him, of Joe's might be, and what he was doing in these parts.

'I wish I could hear what they're saying to each other,' he muttered.

Mr. Tootell's vanity would have hardly been tickled had his wish been gratified, for the stranger's first words to Joe were—

'Why do you stand that prying old fool pottering about the premises?'

CHAPTER II

MORE CATCHES THAN ONE

EXETER versus Exmouth. It is the night before the match, and like the Saxons on the eve of Hastings, the Exeter men are holding high revel—not perhaps the best preparation for the 'twisters' and 'shooters' that await them next day. At present, however, the quaint coffee-room at the Beacon rings with the mirth of as pleasant a party as ever gathered round its centre table, the life and soul of which appears to be a tall, good-looking young fellow, with bold blue eyes and a heavy blonde moustache.

'Well, Fred,' exclaims one of the party, 'we never thought you would turn up in time for the match. You have three or four days' leave left, too.'

'Leave,' said the young man before alluded to; 'what's the use of that when you are regularly cleaned out. Turn up? The only doubt about my turning up was whether I could raise enough money to pay for my ticket; after the dressing we got at Goodwood sovereigns were sovereigns.'

'Yes, I suppose so,' said another of the party. 'I saw by the papers that backers had a bad time of it. I thought of you, Hallaton.'

'Very kind of you,' returned that young gentleman, ' but what recalled my interesting self to your memory?'

'Don't you recollect, when the Colonel

rather hesitated about giving you leave, you said it would be hundreds out of your pocket if he didn't let you go to Goodwood.'

'Ah! yes,' replied Fred Hallaton, laughing. '"Hope springs eternal," &c., and fallacious as we know it, we still cling fondly to the old illusion.'

At one angle of the coffee-room and in close vicinity to the central table was a small recess, which seemed meant for the special accommodation of either a misanthrope or of two people who had something very confidential to say to one another. It was tenanted at present by a gentleman who was dining alone, a dark wirily-built man of medium height with a pair of restless grey eyes. He was apparently absorbed in his dinner, which was of a more luxurious nature than that of his neighbours. He had taken little heed of the badinage of the cricketers until the allusion to Goodwood aroused his attention. As Hallaton's name caught his ear, a smile stole over his face, and he tossed off a glass of champagne with considerable gusto. From the alcove where he was seated he could not see above one or two of his neighbours, and of these Hallaton was not one, but he was a man of excellent memory, and not likely to forget a name which he had written down with much profit to himself so often during the late Goodwood meeting. Sam Mercer indeed was quite as shrewd a business man as his father, but with more dash and go in him than perhaps the elder man had ever had; a keenly observant man, and one who rarely forgot anything that had once come to his knowledge. He rather wanted to learn something about Mr. Hallaton, for as yet all he knew of him was confined to the fact that he was in the Royal Artillery, which information he had gathered from the young gentleman's betting-book, on the cover of which was stamped his name and regiment. He had never met him before the other day, and during the Goodwood week had found him a good customer.

'It would be as well,' thought Sam Mercer, 'to find out what his prospects are; if he is not tinny, he won't last long, considering the way he bet at Goodwood.'

As the cricketing party broke up, Hallaton strolled up the room to look out of the window. As his eye fell on the tenant of the recess, he exclaimed, 'Mercer, by Jove! What on earth are you doing here?'

'Well, Mr. Hallaton, I belong to these parts, and we most of us, as you know, take a bit of a holiday after the Sussex fort-night.'

'Ah,' replied Hallaton, laughingly, 'and you can all afford it this year, which is more than we can. I only hope we shall have better luck to-morrow than I had at Goodwood.'

'Hope you may, sir; at all events, it looks like fine weather.'

Hallaton nodded good-humouredly, and then made his way after his companions to the smoking-room, little thinking what an influence the acquaintance of the bookmaker was destined to have upon his future life.

The match between Exeter and Exmouth always occasioned considerable excitement and attracted a fashionable gathering. The strength of the two elevens was always some-what difficult to estimate, on account of the everchanging element which pervaded both

places. Exmouth was constantly reinforced
by some good cricketers amongst the visitors,
who took temporary service under its banner,
whilst Exeter, if it could not reckon on
gathering strength from visitors, always had
the soldiers to fall back upon, who at times
lent very valuable aid. As the bookmaker
predicted, it was a glorious day, and the
pretty cricket ground was thronged in consequence. The Exmouth men had gone in
first, and disasters fell thick upon them, and
it looked at one time as if they were about
to be disposed of for a very poor score, but
the tail of the eleven discovered unexpected
vitality. One of the visitors who was put in
seventh man developed hitting powers which
he had been far from being credited with.
He fairly collared the bowling, and what that
means at cricket we all know. Bowler after

bowler was tried against him, but his eye was now well in, and he hit them all over the field with apparent ease and satisfaction to himself. His partners, too, had gained courage, and the score ran up apace. Instead of being all out for some seventy or eighty runs, as was at one time threatened, the Exmouth men had quite doubled that score. There was still one wicket to fall, and that seemed hard to get. At one end was the champion, who had come so opportunely to the succour of his side; at the other was a steady and cautious man, who troubled himself nothing about run-getting, but devoted himself solely to the keeping up of his wicket. The bowlers were demoralised, and there seemed no parting this last pair. At last the chance came. Fred Hallaton was scouting deep as 'long field.' Suddenly the champion of the afternoon lifted a half volley, high in the air, and apparently over the heads of the fielders. Amidst shouts of 'well hit,' Hallaton started like a deer in pursuit, and finished the Exmouth innings by as brilliant a one handed catch as ever was seen on that ground. Though never losing hold of the ball, Hallaton had run at such speed that he was unable to stop himself till he blundered right into the benches, which were placed round the boundary. As he threw up the ball, amidst cries of 'well caught' and quite a round of applause, he turned to apologise to a smartly dressed, good-looking young woman, into whose arms he had all but precipitated himself.

'Ten thousand pardons,' he exclaimed, 'but you see he had given us such a deal of trouble. I hope I have done no harm to your dress.'

'Not at all,' replied the young lady with a smile, and flashing a pair of wicked black eyes upon him.

'Well caught, indeed, sir,' said a voice close to him. 'My sister, I am sure, would have forgiven you, Mr. Hallaton, if you had torn her skirts ever so bad, merely to see such a catch made. It looked two to one against us at one time, but I reckon it's even money now.'

'Splendidly fielded. Who is he?' exclaimed a haughty-looking gentleman, who was exhibiting considerable expanse of white waistcoat and heavy gold watch chain in the front row of the seats in the pavilion. 'Hallaton, did you say?' he continued, in reply to one of his neighbours who had furnished him with the name. 'Not Hallaton of the Artillery, is it? Playing for Exeter, no doubt it is! The name is not common. Why, God bless me! I had a letter from his uncle months ago asking me to be civil to him as he was coming to Exeter; but, dear me, I've had so much to do I've never had time to look him up. You recollect my telling you all about it, Mary?'

'No, papa,' replied a slight, fair, ladylike-looking girl who was seated by his side, 'I wish you had. I'd have taken care then that we did the civil to him, and sent him an invitation for something or other.'

'I'll go down and make his acquaintance at once,' and so saying Mr. Lydney bustled down the stairs in search of the hero of the moment.

Mr. Lydney, the prosperous banker of the town, was a very busy man, as well as a wealthy one. He lived in very good style, entertained largely, and nothing went on in Exmouth without his taking a part in it. He subscribed liberally to all the institutions, the cricket club, &c. Mary Lydney, his only child, kept house for him, and it was a marvel to most people that she remained Mary Lydney still. She was very nice-looking, and, there could be no doubt, must inherit a considerable fortune eventually from her father, to say nothing of what he might choose to do during his lifetime if she married with his approval. Curiously enough, she had been twice formally engaged, and the fact had been publicly announced, and yet upon both occasions the affair had been broken off, after having gone on for some time. In neither case had any but the most conventional reason been assigned. The banker only remarked that he supposed Mary had thought better of it, that his daughter must do as she pleased, and that he had no desire to force her inclinations. Now, if Mary Lydney had been a flirt, this would have been easy to understand ; but there never was a girl with less coquetry in her nature. Moreover, those who knew Mary Lydney best declared that in the first instance she had been very much in earnest and most thoroughly in love. Both men had been quite eligible in every respect. True, neither had been rich, but surely in her case that was no great objection. However, so matters stood, and this was as much as any one, except, perhaps, the father and laughter, knew about it.

Mr. Lydney failed in his attempt to find Fred Hallaton. That gentleman, instead of returning to the pavilion, had remained to improve his acquaintance with Miss Mercer.

He had been much struck by the black-browed young beauty, and she, on her part, was never loth to receive the attentions of a new admirer. She was insatiable in her thirst for admiration, excessively proud of her personal appearance, and quite capable of carrying on three or four flirtations at the same time: a woman to whom a man was not likely to become more than a caprice. It is needless to be said that shyness was not one of Miss Mercer's attributes. She conversed readily with Hallaton, and questioned him freely about himself and his pursuits. Her brother, in the course of the morning, had mentioned his meeting with Hallaton on the preceding night at the Beacon Hotel, and also that that gentleman was one of the officers quartered at Exeter. Sarah had never had an officer in her train as yet. She saw that Fred was rather struck, exerted herself to the utmost to captivate him, and succeeded in enchaining the young artillery-man to her side till two or three cries of ' Hallaton ' attracted his attention, and rising in response to these shouts, Fred was curtly adjured by one of his comrades to ' come along and look sharp, as he was the next man to go in.'

' Wish me luck, won't you?' he said, as he prepared to comply with the injunction, ' and don't think that I shall fail to find my way out to the Dragon before long.'

A saucy nod was the sole reply, and shortly afterwards, having donned his armour, Hallaton sallied forth to do battle for Exeter.

Once more Fred Hallaton did his side good service, and though his innings could hardly be described as brilliant, yet it was a useful one, and by the time he returned to the pavilion the match bore a very interesting aspect. Exeter had still three wickets to fall, and were only thirty-seven runs behind their opponents. On entering the pavilion Fred was promptly laid hands on by the banker.

'I must introduce myself, Mr. Hallaton. My name is Lydney, old friend of your Uncle Bob's. Haven't seen him for years, by the way. He wrote to me about you, but I'm ashamed to say I've been so busy lately that I have not been able to look you up. However, I hope you'll come and see us. My daughter shall send you a line ; come up and be introduced to her ; ' and with this the banker carried off Hallaton to the roof of the stand, and introduced him to Mary Lydney. His mind powerfully impressed with the bold black eyes and vivid colouring of Sarah Mercer, Fred's first impression of Miss Lydney was that she was pale and insipid, but he soon discovered that she was a pleasant enough girl to talk to, and that her conversation was not so flavourless as he had been prepared to find it. Mary apologised for her father's oversight, and warmly seconded the invitation.

'I will send you a line to the Barracks with all formalities, Mr. Hallaton, and trust that you will come and see us. Of course, there will be a bed for you. In the meantime, perhaps you will waive ceremony and dine with us to-night?'

But that Fred Hallaton declined to do, and with a courteous hope that Miss Lydney would be present to see the finish of the game on the morrow, Hallaton took his departure, and made the best of his way back to the Beacon Hotel.

CHAPTER III

THE BANKER'S DAUGHTER

MR. SAM MERCER was not wont to stay with
his family during his brief visits to Exmouth.
He invariably put up at the Beacon Hotel.
He was fond of and on excellent terms with
his parents, but his business as a bookmaker
left him but little leisure either for writing or
visiting, and it was no uncommon thing for
months to elapse without any communication
taking place between him and his people.
He had been not a little surprised to hear,
upon his arrival at the Beacon, that his father
had taken the old Dragon Inn. He had seen
the old man dip into all sorts of eccentric

speculations. He knew what a reticent man
he was on all matters of business, but as Sam
said, 'The old 'un generally came out the right
end of the horn.' What this new fad of his
might mean Sam could form no idea, and
whatever his crafty parent's designs might
be, he knew him too well to suppose for one
moment that they would be unfolded to him.
Joe Mercer had a high opinion of his son's
natural astuteness, he had also on a slight
scale tested Sam's business capabilities; when
he was a youngster, about twenty, he had
furnished him with a modest capital and told
him to start for himself. Sam elected to make
his start in America, and it was there that he
still further cultivated a taste for horse-racing
with which he had been always bitten. With
a shrewd head for figures he soon saw there
was money to be made at it, and was toler-

ably successful when out there. But if you mean to make money in business, you must go where business is, and Sam knew that for the professional racing-man there was no country in the world like England. He accordingly returned there, and enrolled himself amongst the noisy fraternity of the ' ring.'

Strong, active, keen-witted, betting on strict mathematical principles, and regarding the losses as mere temporary fluctuations in business, Sam steadily worked his way upwards. He was soon well known as perfectly ' straight,' and acquired a very considerable *clientèle*. His father more than once advanced him money with which to extend his operations, and as Sam in due course repaid such loans he stood high in the old man's estimation. If not one of the leading magnates, Sam Mercer was a thoroughly known man

amidst the members of the mystic circle, a
favourite with most of them, and rather
celebrated for the queer Americanisms with
which he was apt to garnish his conversation.
He had promised to take his sister to see the
finish of the match, and the next morning,
after an early breakfast, Sam wended his way
to the Dragon. There he was cordially welcomed by his own people, and introduced
to a Mr. Brent, who, Sarah informed him as
they walked in the garden afterwards, was a
stranger staying in the house, ' though what
he, father, or any one else can want to stay at
the Dragon for, beats me.'

' Never you mind the old 'un,' rejoined Sam,
' his head is screwed on the right way, I
guess ; but as for this Brent, it is odd, unless
he has come after you, Sallie.'

' He needn't trouble to let me know it if

he has,' replied the girl with a toss of her head.
' 'Tis not likely I'd look at the likes of him.'

' He might think you good-looking, though
you don't think him,' replied her brother,
laughing ; ' but how do you like the move ? '

' Oh, I don't mind it much,' replied Sarah.
' One house is pretty near the same as another,
while we go on in this old pottering way.
I want to go away and begin life afresh.
Everybody says father has got money, and yet
we go on just as we did when we were
supposed to be poor.'

' Ah,' said Sam ; ' you want to splurge about
a bit, keep a carriage, and play the lady ? '

The girl nodded. ' I'm sick of tramping
up and down the Esplanade,' she remarked.
' I want a change of some sort.'

' Never fear. A good-looking young
woman like you will get that before long.

Time we went tramping if we mean to see
the finish of this match.'

On their way into Exmouth Sam suddenly
exclaimed, 'Here's old Tootell; he is certain
to stop us and ask where we're going.'

'He ought not to ask me,' replied Sarah
laughing, 'for the last time he did I told him
bluntly not in his direction. Now, Sam, that
is one of the plagues of keeping an inn. That
dreadful old man is the torment of our lives.
We can't shut the door against him, as we
could before we turned innkeepers. You
know what he is, and he is eternally prying
about the Dragon—comes to see how we're
getting on, he says. What Mr. Brent is doing
here puzzles you; as for Mr. Tootell, it causes
him sleepless nights.'

But upon this occasion, strange to say,
Tootell raised his hat and hurried past

them.   Like many idle men he passed a considerable portion of his time in looking out of
the window, and from that post of vantage
his attention had been attracted a few minutes
previously by the appearance of Mr. Brent
making his way to the very centre of the town.
He had never seen Mr. Brent in Exmouth
before.   What could he want there?   Mr.
Tootell was going up to the cricket ground,
but he considered that if possible to discover
what had brought Mr. Brent into Exmouth of
paramount importance.   To know what his
neighbours were doing, and to ascertain who
and what any stranger might be who turned
up in the town or its outskirts, had become
quite a disease with Mr. Tootell.   Since his
retirement from the 'public' line he had been
deprived of what was to him a source of un-
mitigated enjoyment.   Mr. Tootell had a

great belief in his own powers as a comic
entertainer, and was wont to give specimens
of his talents in that line, to a few of his intimates in his own bar-parlour. These performances were usually received with great
enthusiasm; his songs and recitations met with
much applause, as is wont to be the case when
the host is an entertainer in more ways than one,
and Tootell on such occasions pushed the bowl
about with the generous freedom of the post-
boys in the famous lyric. His exhibitions of the
seasons, in which his face was by turns supposed
to express spring, summer, autumn, and winter,
always brought down the house, and were
the most extraordinary exhibitions of facial
contortion ever seen. Some carping critic, it
is true, had derisively said that if Mr. Tootell
would turn his attention to grinning through
a horse-collar he would be sure of the top

prize in most country fairs.   Be that as it may,
the self-satisfied tones in which he announced
laughing spring, slumberous summer, fitful
autumn, and boisterous winter, and then proceeded to facially illustrate them was a sight
always received with inextinguishable laughter.

Mr. Tootell, indeed, was much given to
theatricals, and never lost an opportunity of
displaying his histrionic powers, and though
people were unkind enough to say that whether
he made up or whether he made faces he was
always Tootell, and an irredeemable stick, yet
that was by no means Mr. Tootell's idea of
his own humour as a low comedian.   It is
necessary to mention his passion for theatricals,
because this taste initiated him to some extent
in the art of making-up, and though he might
perhaps fail in his own person, yet it showed
him how clever actors could disguise them-

selves by the assistance of wigs and pigments;
and this knowledge, as we shall see, was
destined to involve Mr. Tootell in an awkward
predicament. When he met Sam Mercer and
his sister he had for the moment lost sight of
Mr. Brent, and it was his anxiety to once more
hold that gentleman in view that caused him
to pass them so hurriedly. He very soon recovered the trail, and following Brent at a
wary distance, saw him go into an ironmonger's
shop. This circumstance would have hardly
cost any man but Tootell a second thought,
but that worthy, muttering to himself, 'Now,
what can he want there?' stopped on reach-
ing the window and looked in. Brent was
engaged in purchasing some few things,
apparently connected with the innkeeping
trade, such as taps, funnels, &c. Having
obtained these, he put the parcel under his

arm, and coming out of the shop, proceeded
to retrace his steps in the direction of the
Dragon. Mr. Tootell shook his head, and
wended his way to the cricket ground im-
mersed in a brown study. Who was this
man Brent? What was he staying at the
Dragon for, and what the dickens did he want
with taps, funnels, &c.?

'Bought 'em for old Joe Mercer, I s'pose;
old Joe didn't buy things like that for himself;' and once more Mr. Tootell shook his
head, and proceeded in quest of information.

Play was in full swing when he arrived
there, and the match in that interesting con-
dition of being anyone's game. Exmouth
was just finishing their second innings, but
had not done quite so well as in their first
essay; still, for all that, what with having
some few runs in hand on the first innings,

they promised to put the Exeter men in for a very respectable total. A few minutes more and the last Exmouth wicket has fallen, and after the usual pause Exeter sets to work to make the 122 runs necessary to victory. It is almost needless to observe that Mr. Tootell was more absorbed in watching the doings of his neighbours than in watching the cricket.

'Hallo,' he muttered to himself, 'who's that young spark that Sallie Mercer has got hold of? Handsome girl, Sallie, but she must be getting on. Let me see, how old is she?'

Mr. Tootell was a peripatetic chronological table, or as the young ladies of his acquaintance expressed it, 'an old horror about dates.' But his thoughts on Miss Mercer's age were dissipated by his running against a fellow gossip from Exeter—something of his own kidney—and from him he immediately sought the information he wanted about Miss Mercer's cavalier.

'That,' returned the other, 'that is Mr. Hallaton, the young officer who made the great catch yesterday for Exeter. He seems a little caught himself just now, doesn't he?'

'Ah! you've got quite a new lot of officers this year in Exeter, haven't you? How d'ye do, Mr. Mercer, we were just talking about the officers in Exeter, and you were saying, Mr. Wilson——'

'That we have got a very lively lot this time.'

'Throw their money about freely, eh?' said Sam, 'and keep the tambourine a-rolling. It must make a good deal of difference to the town what sort of set you have at the barracks.'

'Yes,' replied Wilson, 'sometimes they are

a much more moneyed lot than others, and of
course that makes a difference.'

'And those you've got there now are full
of money?' inquired Sam.

'Just so,' replied Wilson. 'There's young
Hallaton and two or three more of 'em must
spend a deal of money one way and the other.'

Sam Mercer passed on with a careless nod,
and left the two old gossips to exchange
scandal at their leisure. Young Hallaton at
all events had the reputation of being well off
in the town where he was quartered, and this
was a little bit of information that Mercer was
glad to acquire, as he trusted to henceforth
number young Hallaton amongst his customers. Not that he had any sinister designs
against that young gentleman, but if he was
destined to lose his money over racing, it might
as well go into his, Sam Mercer's, pockets, as

anyone else's, and he thought Fred Hallaton far too excitable a young man not to find the turf a very expensive pursuit before he was much older.

Mr. Hallaton devoted himself pretty well to Miss Mercer nearly the entire afternoon, and Sarah was nothing loth to parade her admirer before the eyes of Exmouth then and there assembled. In fact, when his innings came and he returned to the pavilion without making much addition to the score, his bosom ally, Dicky Chives, could not resist chaffing him about his flirtation.

'Look here, young man,' said Dicky, ' flirting is all right and regular, but there are times and seasons for it. You can't expect to play cricket and flirt as outrageously as you have been doing. You would never have muffed that ball if you had been cool, and in your right mind. Of course you were thinking how you would astonish that handsome girl, in whose pocket you have been sitting all the afternoon, and you did !'

'Shut up, Dicky,' was the laughing rejoinder, ' we all play a little too slow at 'em sometimes.'

'More especially when we are wool gathering, as you were,' said Chives. 'Mark me, young fellow,' he continued with mock solemnity, ' your passion for petticoats will be your ruin.'—'There he goes again,' soliloquised Dicky, as Fred ran up the stairs leading to the roof to shake hands with Miss Lydney. 'He can't keep away from 'em,' and with that Mr. Chives hurried to the refreshment bar to calm his feelings.

Dicky Chives was a well-known man in the Royal Artillery, and an athlete of no mean description. Usually captain of their cricket team wherever he was quartered, and always engaged in boating and racquet-playing, shooting, or something of that description, he held curiously aloof from feminine society. Popular and well known amongst men, he was never seen in a ball-room, and when his brother officers thought to return hospitalities they had received in that fashion, it was declared that Dicky, although ready enough to put his hand in his pocket, invariably applied for three days' leave, until, to use his own expression, 'the shine was over.'

'Sorry for your bad luck, personally, Mr. Hallaton,' said Mary Lydney, as she shook hands, 'but my sympathies, of course, are all with Exmouth—a most interesting match. Three wickets to fall. Oh, no! There goes another, and Exeter wants forty-one runs to win yet.'

'And will never get it,' exclaimed the banker. 'It will be a close finish, but we shall just pull through. I shall be broke,' he continued, laughing, 'if we don't. I've got a sovereign on Exmouth.'

'We shall bring your heart in your mouth yet,' rejoined Hallaton, smiling. 'The last two wickets often give a deal of trouble.'

Fred's careless words came true in the present instance, and Exeter crept up within thirteen runs of their opponents before their stumps were scattered for the last time, and Exmouth was left the victor by that amount.

'A capital match,' exclaimed the banker; 'and mind, Hallaton, you have promised to pay us a visit next week.'

'All right, I am not likely to forget Miss Lydney's commands.' And so saying, Fred raised his straw hat and rejoined his comrades.

CHAPTER IV

' THE OLD BALL-ROOM '

' So you are off to-morrow, Sam,' said Miss Mercer to her brother, as he walked home with her after the cricket match ; ' how I wish I was ! '

' Well, I guess you've no cause to complain,' he replied. 'You had a pretty good time to-day, anyhow. That young Hallaton was " saloon- ing " you about pretty well the whole after- noon. You seemed to take to him rather kindly.'

' I should rather have said that he took kindly to me,' retorted the girl, laughing. ' Yes, he is rather nice. I wonder whether he has got any money.' These officers I've heard say are seldom rich, for all their laced jackets.'

'They have a good bit of money, some of them,' replied her brother, 'I know, because I have dealings with them. This young Hallaton, I fancy, is well off; but it's not likely to matter much to you. No doubt he admires you, but a swell like him is not likely to come to the Dragon for a wife.'

'That's so like a brother,' replied the girl pettishly. 'I'm sure I wish we had never come to the old tumbledown place. One hears such queer noises there at night. I declare, if I believed in ghosts I should think it was haunted.'

'Queer noises,' said Sam, 'odd, what sort of noises?'

'Oh! I don't know, the whole place creaks. It's only the windows or rats, I suppose.'

'I shall say good-bye to you here,' said Sam. 'I said it to the old folks this morning. Is there anything wrong with mother, by the way? She's got a worried, anxious look about her that she didn't use to have.'

'Nothing that I know of,' rejoined the girl.

'My fancy, perhaps,' replied her brother, as he kissed her, and then, turning on his heel, he strolled back to his hotel.

Miss Mercer walked on towards the Dragon, excessively pleased with herself and all the world. She had had a good-looking young officer dangling at her side before the public nearly the whole of the afternoon. She was conscious of looking her best, and that her proceedings had been viewed by her friends with envy and all uncharitableness. She smiled to herself as she fancied she heard the expressions—'Forward thing!' and 'Look how that Sallie Mercer is carrying on!' Miss Mercer was no innocent girl in her teens, but a young woman who knew the world. She might not be accomplished, but she was as quick-witted as any of her family, and less burdened with principle. She had no pitiable weakness, for instance, about adhering to the truth if she considered a lie would serve her purpose better. Just the sort of woman whose fatal beauty lures men to their undoing. She threw her head up proudly as she thought of her brother's remark. 'Not come to the Dragon for a wife, indeed,' she muttered. 'Sam don't know much about women, or else he'd not talk foolish like that. There's plenty will come to the Dragon, or anywhere else when Sallie Mercer lifts up her finger,' and then she began to reflect that though it was undoubtedly true that she might have been married more than once, yet it was equally certain that she had never as yet hooked a fish she considered worth landing. As for young Hallaton, he had promised to come out and see her at the Dragon, and let Sam think what he might, if she could only see a little more of that gentleman, she fancied that the result would be in her own hands.

Sam, on his part, as he walked back to the Beacon, dismissed all thought of young Hallaton from his mind. 'I dare say,' he reflected, ' that Sallie does get a little tired of the old jog-trot life. It's all very well for a few days rest, but it would kill me in a month. However, peace and happiness ain't much in the way of a regular racing man, and the cry of " I'll take six to four " beats the songs of the thrushes and the blackbirds into fits! It's a rum start what made the old 'un take that inn; however, he knows what he is about, and is more likely to have an ace up his sleeve than expose his hand,' and then Sam Mercer went into the Beacon to snatch a hasty dinner before catching the night mail to town.

Country quarters from time immemorial have enjoyed an unenviable notoriety for the facility they afford those quartered in them of getting into scrapes, and it was not likely that the metropolis of the West was going to prove an exception. Fred Hallaton had been unmistakably smitten by the belle of the Dragon. He had a good deal of idle time on his hands; Exmouth and Exeter were by rail but twenty minutes apart, and two days after the cricket match saw Fred Hallaton making his way out to call on Miss Mercer. That young lady received him with the sweetest of smiles.

'Ah, this is good of you, Mr. Hallaton,' she exclaimed, as she extended her hand. 'You men are very apt to promise to come and see us, and then forget all about us till we next help you to kill an idle afternoon.'

'I can't fancy anyone forgetting you,' replied Fred, with an ardent glance. 'I was so much interested in your account of this old inn, that I thought I would take advantage of your promise to show it me.'

'I don't know that there's much to show,' returned the girl. 'It is more the stories connected with it; but I'll show you one room running out at the back which really is curious.'

She led the way up a few stairs, then along a passage, then down a few stairs again at the other end, threw open a door, and said— 'This is the ball-room.'

' Ball-room ! ' ejaculated Hallaton, ' and what on earth does an inn like the Dragon want with a ball-room ? '

' Well,' replied Sarah, ' the house is a good big one, as you see, and years and years ago people used to come out from Exmouth in the summer time and dance here.'

It was a good-sized room, quite capable of containing a party of four or five score people for dancing purposes. At one end was a much-out-of-repair little music gallery. Joe Mercer had evidently not thought it worth while to go to any expense about doing up this part of the house. There was lots of old furniture heaped up about it, broken chairs, benches, &c., and it was pervaded with that peculiar smell which characterises a room in which the windows are never opened ; the dust of many years had accumulated on the rickety furniture, which had probably been taken over by tenant after tenant, when the palmy days of the Dragon had departed. It was evidently many years since the room had been used in any way.

'The old people about,' continued Sarah, 'declare that there used to be no end of fun and capers going on here when they were young; that there were lots of dances went on during the summer months, and in the winter they say it was given up to the smugglers, who used to drink and smoke and carry on all sorts of mad games. There's an old fellow here, oh, ever so old, over eighty, I'm sure, to whom I sometimes go and talk when I'm dull, who tells horrible tales about what went on at the Dragon when he was young; all lies, I dare say.'

'Ah! I don't know,' replied Hallaton.

'I fancy there was a good deal of wild work went on along these coasts in those times. Smuggling was at its height then, and I should think those who followed it were a pretty rough lot.'

'Yes, old Mutter tells dreadful tales about the Dragon. Perhaps he only does it to frighten me. He says the smugglers when they got mad with drink, would quarrel amongst themselves and use their knives and pistols on one another. He declares he has seen more than one man carried out of this room dead, and he's got a horrible story of an adventurous exciseman who got in amongst the smugglers, in disguise, but was discovered before he could get back to his comrades with the information he had gained, and was never heard of afterwards.'

'And what did people say became of him?'

asked Hallaton, who was getting much interested in the legends of the Dragon, or, it
might be, in the narrator of them, who was
looking extremely handsome in her pink
cambric morning dress.

'He was murdered, old Mutter declares.
However, I know I wouldn't come into this
room at night, and I don't believe in ghosts,
either.   But there's something uncanny
about it.   Look,' she added, ' do you see this
trap-door in the corner?   They say that leads
down to where the smugglers used to stow
their brandy and stuff.'

'Has anybody ever been down to see?'
asked Hallaton.

'Father did, when he first took the house.
He says there are only a couple of large
cellars which haven't been used for a long
time.   But come out into the sunshine; this
old room always gives me the creeps.'

As they went towards the door Hallaton's eye was suddenly caught by a candlestick, a box of lucifer matches and a short clay pipe, which were lying on a rickety table not very far from the trap-door.

'The only sign of the days we live in,' he exclaimed, laughing, as he touched the lucifers with his stick.

'Odd,' said Sarah. 'I wonder who has been into the room. I'm sure neither of the two girls would enter if you paid them for it. I suppose it must have been father for something or other.'

They passed out of the room, and Miss Mercer led the way to the garden, where the conversation speedily took a more personal turn. Sarah had every reason to feel confident that she had not over-estimated her attractions. Fred Hallaton wandered about the garden with her for the best part of an hour, and was then formally presented to her parents as 'Mr. Hallaton, a friend of Sam's.'

Fred rather winced at this. Sam Mercer was, no doubt, a very respectable man in his line, but his acquaintanceship with Hallaton certainly did not justify his being described as one of that gentleman's 'friends.' Yet the girl had but cleverly taken advantage of the fact that it was her brother who had introduced Fred to her. Joe Mercer welcomed him with the greatest cordiality, insisted upon his having a glass of ale, said it was a queer old inn, and there was a many strange tales told about it.

'I don't trouble my head about it myself, but Sarah there has a taste for these bygone tales. You must come over and see us again,

sir, and get her to take you down the road
a bit to old Mutter's. He will spin you
yarns by the hour about it. I shouldn't
wonder if old Bob had seen a sight or two in
these walls he'd as lieve not speak about.'

'Thanks,' replied Fred, as he swallowed
his ale and prepared to go. 'I shall take
an early opportunity of coming over again;
these smuggling legends always interest me,
and you have promised to be my cicerone,
Miss Mercer.'

She wasn't very clear what that was, but
she nodded assent and flashed her black eyes
up into his face as she accompanied him to
the gate.

'Good-bye,' she said. 'Don't forget to
come soon, and I'll take you down to see old
Mutter. Only give the old man a little
tobacco, and a trifle to buy rum with, and

he'll go on yarning as long as you care to listen to him.' And then, with a quick little nod, she turned back to the house.

Fred Hallaton was conscious of having passed a very pleasant afternoon as he strode back on his way towards the railway-station. As he neared his goal he encountered a fussy little man, who, after eyeing him with evident interest, suddenly took off his hat, and asked him if he could tell him what o'clock it was. As the stranger was palpably wearing a watch, at all events a chain, Fred thought it rather singular that he should make this request, and as he took out his own watch to comply with it, observed dryly, 'I suppose yours don't go!'

'Well, yes, it does,' stammered the stranger, 'but, but not quite, with the—accuracy necessary'—and here the speaker's voice swelled, as of a man at last safely delivered of his lie—'to the happiness of a man of punctual habits——'

'Half-past five, and I recommend you to look sharp,' said Hallaton, with a steady stare at his questioner. 'I should think your friends would be anxious to see you.'

'Yes,' replied Mr. Tootell, for he of course was the stranger. 'Poor old Joe Mercer looks to seeing me pretty well every day; and capital good ale at the Dragon, ain't it, sir?'

'How the devil should I know?' returned Hallaton so sharply that Mr. Tootell involuntarily took a step or two backwards.

'No offence,' he replied, deprecatingly. 'I don't mean any harm, I'm sure, but old Joe does keep good ale, and Sallie is an uncommon fine gal.'

'I don't know who you are, or where you

may be going,' rejoined Fred fiercely, ' but
I recommend you, wherever it is, to go, for
if you pester me any more with your confounded remarks I'll chuck you down the
next area we come across.'

' Oh, I don't want to intrude upon anyone,
especially the servants,' rejoined Mr. Tootell,
drawing himself up in a way that provoked a
smile from Fred Hallaton's lips ; ' but I thought
perhaps you were friendly with the Mercers.'

' Well, never mind what you thought,'
rejoined Fred, ' my way lies here, and yours,
no doubt, in some other direction.'

' Oh, I don't mind which way I walk ; my
time's at my own disposal ; if you're going to
the station, I'll just look in and see how my
watch tallies with the station clock. Perhaps
you have a train to catch ? If both our
tickers were wrong it will be a case of " Oh,

what a surprise!"' and Mr. Tootell was
proceeding to warble a strain of the popular
refrain, when Hallaton turned sharply upon
him, and said, 'You had better take your
musical talents, sir, where they will be appre-
ciated; in the meanwhile, I wish you good
afternoon.'

Mr. Tootell stopped; this was an insult to
his vocal ability which he could not overlook.
Moreover, as he admitted afterwards, 'That
tall young man looked dangerous.' 'Huffy,'
he remarked to himself; 'these military gents
are apt to be supercilious. Now, I wonder if
he has been out to the Dragon?'

CHAPTER V

TOOTELL IS PUZZLED

' I don't understand it and I don't quite like it,' said Mrs. Mercer dogmatically, as she sat in the Dragon bar-parlour conversing with her husband and Mr. Brent.

'Well, I don't much like it myself,' replied Joe. 'It's rather too risky a speculation for my taste.

'Nonsense!' said Brent, 'who's to suspect you? Did you ever make so much money in the time before? Business is just in full swing now. Another eighteen months and our fortune is made.'

'That's all true enough,' rejoined Mercer,

' but it's a dangerous game, and I wish I had
never started on it.'

' Stuff and nonsense!' retorted Brent, ' we
won't go into particulars. Who risks most, I
should like to know—you or I?'

' That don't very much matter,' said Joe.
' When you are busted, it don't signify how
much you're busted.'

' Come, come,' said Brent soothingly, ' it's
no use funking now. You've sailed as close
to the wind many a time, I'll be bound.'

' Never!' said the other emphatically, as
he brought his fist down on the table. ' I've
not been over particular, I admit, but I never
went as far as this before. It's all very well;
you've been playing a game of hide and seek
all your life—I haven't; there has never been
anything against me that I couldn't face.'

' Oh, come!' rejoined Brent, ' you needn't

go bragging about your character now.
Remember, if you cut the whole business to-
morrow you are in just the same scrape as if
you carried on for another year or so. I'm
not a rich man, and have got too much money
in this business to drop such a paying concern.
You *must* go on.'

'That's true, missis,' said Joe, turning to
his wife; 'I'll back out as soon as I can, but
it can't be yet.'

'Just so,' said Brent; 'now look here,
we've been a little imprudent trusting to the
ghost stories to keep the girls out of the old
ball-room. We've been weak enough to leave
the key in the lock. There is nobody but the
maids, I suppose, ever goes near it?'

'No,' replied Mrs. Mercer, 'and neither of
them dare go inside, I'll pound it.'

'It was Dan's turn on, so I wasn't down-

stairs. He said he heard voices in the ball-
room this afternoon. It is well I had a special
key made. That door must be kept locked
in future.'

'I can't think who it could have been,'
said Mercer, whose face betrayed unmistak-
able signs of uneasiness, 'but I'll take good
care that the room is kept locked in future.'
And here the appearance of Sarah with an
inquiry as to whether supper was ready put
an end to the conversation.

Fred Hallaton on his way home to Exeter
became suddenly conscious of a violent desire
to learn all that he could about the coast lore
of Devonshire. He determined to set to work
and pick up all the smuggling legends he
could lay his hands on, and those connected
with the old Dragon Inn in particular, but he
did not think proper to dilate on his newly

acquired information for the benefit of his brother officers at dinner that evening. On the contrary, when questioned about his proceedings by his particular chum, Dicky Chives, he was peculiarly reticent concerning them, and was so unusually silent that that worthy at last remarked dryly, ' that whatever he had been doing, it didn't seem to have agreed with him.'

Young men in Fred Hallaton's state are either apt to be silent, or, worse still, garrulous, and then, as most of us have painful experience, they wax eloquent only on the one subject. Hallaton had attained his twenty-fifth year, and this was the first time he had ever been seriously attracted by a woman's charms. He had spent only two afternoons in Sarah's society and was already entangled in a desperate flirtation with that young lady.

In considerable danger, if he only knew it, of making an arrant fool of himself. The game was too uneven, he was over head and ears in love with her, whilst Sarah, though about his own age, was years older in all knowledge of affairs of the heart. If her flirtations had been numerous no one of them had cost her a regret. It was the cool calculating player against the impetuous novice. Needless to add that the game was in the former's hands and that the latter would be eventually at her mercy, hers to do what she willed with, to toss on one side or to take to herself as a husband.

Chives, however, at the present had not the slightest suspicion that his comrade was so stricken; he often chaffed Fred about being 'a lady's man,' but that meant no more than that Hallaton was a ball-goer, fond of society, and not afraid of a woman when he met one. Dicky Chives knew in his heart that he was; he would have stood up without flinching to the biggest rough if he had insulted him, but to converse with a lady always threw Dicky into a state of nervous bewilderment. He had seen Hallaton paying great attention to a handsome girl during the cricket match, but he had no idea of who Sarah was or what was her station. To see Fred doing cavalier was no new sight, and though he laughingly predicted that his weakness that way would prove his ruin, Mr. Chives really thought his chum perfectly well able to take care of himself, and would have manifested much incredulity if anybody had suggested that Hallaton was in a fair way to get himself into a terrible scrape. However, it was little likely that Fred's visits to the

Dragon would cease at present, nor was it likely that they would be long before they came to the knowledge of Dicky Chives.

But there was another person who suspected the continuation of the flirtation that he had seen commenced on Exmouth Cricket Ground, and that was Mr. Tootell. Anything of that kind was a perfect godsend to the old gossip, who since his retirement from business had taken the supervision of all the love-making in Exmouth under his own care, and had in consequence run more than one narrow escape of being kicked for his pains. People are sometimes misunderstood ; but Mr. Tootell's unappeasable curiosity was quite understanded by the people of Exmouth. He was dying to know if anything more had come of that promising beginning, and when he had seen Hallaton coming from the direction of the Dragon, he had done his best to learn from him whether he had been there. If this was so it would make the inn highly interesting. He could see how old Joe Mercer was getting on, and superintend Sarah's little affair at the same time. He rubbed his hands with satisfaction ; but here the 'something bitter' arose, as he reflected that they were desperately impetuous young people to meddle with. Mr. Hallaton's manner, he could but acknowledge, upon the one occasion on which he had spoken to him, had been far from friendly, while Miss Mercer, he knew of old, was dangerous to interfere with.

Still the master passion triumphed, and heedless of the unpleasant consequences that had more than once attended his putting his nose into other people's affairs, Mr. Tootell haunted the Dragon more persistently than ever. No rebuff seemed to daunt him, although Mrs. Mercer would storm at him on the slightest provocation, although Sarah barely acknowledged his salutation, and although even Joe himself was as near morose as it was possible for him to be. Mr. Tootell bore it all with imperturbable good temper ; he was not to be irritated ; he came persistently morning after morning, sat for the best part of an hour over his pipe and mild ale, inquiring about every conceivable topic, from how the potatoes were getting on in the garden, to how trade was doing at the bar, to when Sarah was going to be married, to what Mr. Brent was doing down there.

'How should I know?' replied Joe Mercer testily one morning. 'As long as a customer pays his bill, it is nothing to me what his reasons may be for stopping in my house.'

'Well, but what should you think they were?' pertinaciously inquired Tootell.

'I don't bother my head about it,' replied Joe. 'I wonder you don't try the ale at some other hotel occasionally.'

'Rather ungrateful of you that, Joe. You know I promised you when you took the Dragon that you should have the benefit of all my experience, and you shall.'

'I'm not aware that I ever came to you for advice.'

'No, no, you wouldn't, Joe. You're a strong-willed man, with a shrewd head on your shoulders, that's what you are. You don't want everybody's advice about what you're going to do, not you; but for all that, it's the duty of your friends, when you go into a business you don't know anything about, to stand by you.'

'Confound it!' said Mercer. 'I know perfectly well what I'm about. I don't require your advice, nor anyone else's.'

For that morning, at all events, Mr. Tootell was silenced, and finished his ale without making further inquiry. But he had not the slightest intention of abandoning his investigations, and was as determined as ever to find out what business it was that detained Mr. Brent in the neighbourhood, and whether young Hallaton was a constant visitor at the Dragon. He had never met the latter there, and to his interrogations on the subject, both Joe and his wife professed complete ignorance of that gentleman's identity. 'We serve no one of that name,' had been Mercer's reply; 'but it is not to be supposed that I know the name of everybody who comes in for a glass of ale.' To which Mr. Tootell had replied tartly that they weren't so very numerous as to confuse a man's recollection. He suspected that the Mercers were not quite telling the truth, and in this we know he was well justified : but what are you to do with a man of this description ? one might as well publish one's private affairs in the paper as make Mr. Tootell acquainted with them. In his thirst for information on this point, he had at length mustered up courage to inquire of Miss Mercer if she had met Mr. Hallaton lately ; but that young lady rose to the occasion, and with a scornful toss of her head promptly replied, ' If you'll ask me no questions I'll tell you no lies,' and, case-hardened as he was, Mr. Tootell did not dare to pursue the subject further. Miss Mercer was one of

the few people of whom he stood in awe.
Brent, too, Mr. Tootell saw but little of; he
occasionally found that mysterious stranger
in the bar when he visited the Dragon, but
any attempt to inveigle Brent into conversation was hopeless. He was apparently a
walking monosyllable, and the advent of Mr.
Tootell seemed to be to him a signal for
leaving the room. Gradually there stole
upon the former a sort of shadowy idea that
he had seen Brent before at some far away
time; long ago, if it was so, and when or
where it was he had no conception. Although a great slice' of his life had been
passed in Exmouth, yet he had begun the
world in London, and it was the profits he
had made in the ' public' line there that had
enabled him to take the house in Exmouth
where he finally acquired his competency.

This idea once got into his head, Mr. Tootell cudgelled his brain ceaselessly as to who Brent was in the past, and as to where he had met him. He endeavoured to throw himself in his way on every occasion, but the opportunities vouchsafed him were few, and even when he did succeed in pouncing on his victim, Brent speedily made his escape. Save the one occasion upon which he had seen him in Exmouth, he had never encountered Brent except either in, or in the immediate vicinity of, the Dragon. It was all a haze, and he could make nothing of it. One thing only was clear to Mr. Tootell, to wit, if ever he had met Brent in former days that was not the name he then went by ; that he had never known anyone so called he was perfectly certain. That he never encountered Hallaton was due chiefly to the fact that whereas Mr. Tootell usually frequented the Dragon in the morning, Fred generally paid his visits to Sarah in the afternoon, and partly to the mere accident that he had never as yet run across Hallaton on his way to and from the station. Hallaton's journeys to Exmouth had not as yet attracted the attention of his brother officers. It was supposed that he had friends in the town, having been seen talking to Miss Lydney in the cricket pavilion, and the banker was not only a prominent feature in his own town, but was well known in Exeter besides.

'Mercer,' exclaimed Brent, as he entered the bar-parlour hurriedly, soon after the termination of one of Mr. Tootell's visits, 'we must put a stop to that inquisitive old idiot coming here. We've got enough custom just to be the blind we want, and our customers are all of the right sort—men who come in simply for their drinks and a short rest, and nothing else, bar two. I don't much like that young officer coming here. However, there's no mistake about *why* he comes. He is after your daughter and, I'm bound to say, don't seem to have eyes for anything else.'

'Well, Sarah can take care of herself,' replied Mercer; 'so never mind that part of it. He's a good sort, he don't want to know anything, he's no harm about the place, and you can't expect the girl *not* to have a sweet-heart.'

'Oh, I don't so much mind young Hallaton,' returned Brent, 'but we must put a stop to that fellow Tootell coming here. I'd knock his head off for twopence.'

'Oh, yes,' rejoined Joe, 'and there are times when I get so mad with his questioning I could shake the life out of the wretched little atomy, although I've known him the last twenty years and more. But what good would that do? He's a vindictive little devil if he's thwarted, and he'd have either of us up at Exmouth for assault. It only calls attention to the house; and then it wouldn't suit either of us to be turned inside out by one of these lawyer chaps.'

' No,' said Brent, ' it wouldn't suit my book to be in a witness-box at all. One never can tell what licence the beaks would allow a sharp lawyer.'

' He'd not mind either,' said Joe, with a twinkle in his eye ; ' that Tootell wouldn't mind a black eye or so to find out what has brought you down here.'

' No ; as you say, it would draw attention to the house, more or less, and that's just what we don't want. I must devise some other scheme.'

CHAPTER VI

AN EMBARRASSING SALUTE

An invitation to spend a couple of days with the Lydneys reached Fred Hallaton in due course, and as that gentleman had nothing particular to do he resolved to accept it. He thought he could indulge his infatuation for Sarah Mercer quite as easily from the banker's house as from the barracks. His mornings would probably be at his own disposal, and it would be only paying his devotions before noon instead of after. The banker had a capital house standing in very pretty grounds in the outskirts of the town, and here Hallaton and his portmanteau were deposited just in time to dress for dinner. When—after making his toilet—he descended to the drawing-room, he found several people already assembled there. Mr. Lydney kept a capital cook, and prided himself on his little dinners, and not without reason. He was one of those genial hosts who at once set their guests at ease, and without being particularly brilliant, have the knack of setting the ball of conversation going. Though celebrated for his wine, the banker was not remarkable for either witty epigram or sparkling anecdote, but he possessed the invaluable gift of tact. You must have been very dull or hopelessly shy to find yourself left out of the conversasation at Mr. Lydney's table.

Fred found himself placed on his hostess's right. The banker's wife had been dead for some years, and Mary Lydney had long taken the head of her father's table. As it had fallen to his lot to take in a lady, with whom the making of conversation was a toilsome and arduous duty, he not unnaturally turned to his neighbour on the other side. There he, at all events, had no cause to complain, and Fred was soon chatting gaily and pleasantly enough.

'I came across a most extraordinary old lunatic here the other day,' he remarked. 'He stopped me to ask the time, having a watch on himself, and then proceeded to cross-examine me as to where I had been and where I was going. A little, thin, wizened old man, in a tall straw hat. Can you identify him by that description, Miss Lydney?'

Mary burst out laughing. 'Papa,' she exclaimed, 'please listen to this. Now, Mr. Hallaton, please repeat your little story. I think you'll find your friend is pretty well known.'

Fred accordingly reiterated his story, and as he finished a laugh ran round the table and 'Tootell' burst from several lips.

'Tootell!' exclaimed Fred, 'who, and what is he?'

'Quite a character in Exmouth,' said the banker, while the words 'horrid old wretch' escaped his daughter's lips, and such comments as 'insufferable old bore,' 'intolerable nuisance,' &c., fell from others of the party.

'Why, surely,' rejoined Fred, 'he can't annoy any of you, he has no pretensions to be a gentleman? What do you mean?'

'No, no,' replied Mr. Lydney, 'he is only a retired innkeeper, and a chartered bugbear, a regular Old Man of the Sea, that Exmouth can't shake off. He is a most respectable man, and very respectful, but his uncontrollable desire to pry into his neighbours' affairs gets him into all manner of scrapes.'

'I should rather think so,' said Fred.

'Yes,' remarked Miss Lydney, 'and his age and diminutive stature, as a rule, get him out of them. Men get very angry with him, but they can't beat such a little creature as that, tiresome as he is,' and then the conversation drifted into other channels. When the ladies left the room, the men drew up to their host's end of the table.

'I rode past the old Dragon Inn to-day,' remarked one of the guests, as he helped himself to a bumper of the banker's claret. 'You, like myself, Lydney, can recollect it as an inn for many years, though its prosperous times were before our day.'

'Yes, though I can recollect it in my boyhood as a house that did a respectable business, and I've heard my father tell all sorts of queer tales that were current about it when he was a young man. I know he said that more than once, when out picnicking there, he had danced in the old ball-room.'

'Well, I never thought to see it become an inn again,' said the first speaker, 'and what possessed any man to try such a hopeless experiment, I can't conceive.'

'I don't know that it is so very hopeless,' rejoined Mr. Lydney.

'I can't fancy it otherwise,' rejoined the other. 'There's not much money to be gathered from a few chance passers-by.'

'Ah, well,' replied the banker, 'old Mercer is making money somehow or other, though I don't pretend to know how.'

The next morning, after breakfast, Fred

Hallaton had arranged in his own mind to pay a visit to the object of his affections; but we are rarely our own masters in other people's houses, and upon this occasion Fred's scheme was quietly knocked on the head by Mary Lydney.

'Now, Mr. Hallaton,' she said, as they rose from the breakfast table, 'if you will get your letters written, that is, if you have any to write, or your cigar smoked if you have not, I shall be ready to go out with you about eleven, and we will take a turn on the sea-wall, and see if we can beat up some recruits for lawn-tennis this afternoon.'

There was no help for it; there was no possibility of backing out of the challenge of his hostess. He could only reply that he had no correspondence to trouble him, and was quite at her disposal whenever she chose, and

shortly afterwards he found himself prome-
nading the sea-wall. Miss Lydney, it need
be scarcely said, knew pretty well everybody
worth knowing in Exmouth. She stopped to
chat to several of her friends, and Fred found
himself making the acquaintance of half the
young ladies in the town. Having enlisted
her recruits for the afternoon, Miss Lydney
turned her steps homewards, and as they
walked down the Esplanade for the last time
Fred suddenly found himself face to face with
Miss Mercer. Sarah was dressed very simply,
and in good taste. An amused expression
played for a moment over her face, as she
caught sight of Hallaton, and as they passed
she saluted Fred with a malicious smile and
bow. He raised his hat, and the next minute
became conscious of an extremely surprised
expression on his companion's countenance.

'I had no idea, Mr. Hallaton,' she observed, somewhat frigidly, ' that you were acquainted with that lady.'

Fred muttered something confusedly about having been introduced to her in the cricket field, to which Miss Lydney replied a little sharply—'I should have hardly thought that necessary in her case,' and then abruptly changed the subject. Mary, indeed, was very angry ; she of course knew Sarah very well by sight, and was perfectly aware who the handsome, bold-eyed young woman was. She also knew that she was the daughter of a man of humble origin, who had prospered in Exmouth, made a bit of money, and after trying his hand at a good many trades, had finally settled down as an innkeeper. Mary would have described Miss Mercer as a forward minx. She had marked the malicious smile that had spread over her face, and rightly considered it·was a piece of studied impertinence her bowing to a gentleman with whom she was walking, and deemed that, by returning her salute, Fred Hallaton had abetted Miss Mercer's offence. Fred rose at once to the emergency, and began without delay to talk rapidly on some other subject.

Sarah had been quite as keen to note Miss Lydney's annoyance, and started on her way home with a mixture of anger and triumph in her heart. She was pleased at having mortified ' that stuck-up Miss Lydney,' as she called her, but she did not quite approve of Fred's walking about Exmouth with anyone but herself. Not that this had ever happened, for Fred would have fought rather shy at present of parading the town with a young lady in Miss Mercer's position. When she reached her home she found her father and Brent talking in front of the house.

'Do you expect that young soldier chap out to-day,' inquired Joe, idly. 'He wasn't out yesterday, so I suppose it's likely he'll be here to-day?'

'I think not,' replied Sarah, 'for I passed Mr. Hallaton on the Esplanade this morning, and my gentleman seemed half-ashamed to acknowledge me; but I wasn't going to have that, you know.'

'What do you mean?' inquired her father.

'Why, he was walking with that Miss Lydney, who gives herself such airs—whether because she thinks herself good-looking or because her father is so rich, I don't know. He looked as if he were going to pass me without raising his hat, but I made him such a marked bow he was forced to return it. You should have seen Miss Lydney's face, conceited thing. She can't get a husband herself, and can't bear any young man she knows to look at another girl.'

'Do you mean to say,' said Joe, in rather awestruck tones, 'that you bowed to him while he was walking with Miss Lydney?'

'Of course I did,' replied Sarah. 'You don't suppose I will allow a man to know me in one place and not in another?'

'Quite right,' interposed Brent. 'You are a girl of some spirit, you are. So young Hallaton is intimate with the Lydneys, is he?'

'He knows them,' replied Sarah; 'though I should think that is a thing that doesn't much concern you.'

'Rather a quick-tongued young lady,'

remarked Brent, as Sarah swept her way into the house.

'Takes after her mother a bit,' said Joe. 'You'd best speak 'em fair if you want things to go comfortable.'

'Things can't be better than they are,' said Brent. 'As I said before, all that I wish is that we could hit upon some means of getting shot of Tootell, and I own I don't see my way to that.'

'No,' rejoined Joe, sententiously. 'If you keep an inn you can't shut your doors,' and with that the two men turned back into the house.

William Brent was a man who for more than thirty years had been chasing fortune through illicit by-ways, seeking phantasmal riches by various illegal short cuts. If the law had never laid him by the heels it was

owing to his cunning and good luck, and not
because he had not more than once risked
falling into its clutches.   It could not be said
that the police knew him, for that was exactly
what they did not.   Had they been acquainted
with his personality he would not have enjoyed that immunity from the consequences
of the nefarious life he had so long led.   But
if they did not know him by sight they
certainly knew of him, and 'Slippery Bill'
was chronicled on their records as chief pro-
moter and designer of many a clever scheme
for cozening the British Public, and wheed-
ling their hard-earned gains out of their
pockets.   Like all men of his class Brent was
a shrewd judge of human nature.   A desire
to make money with a minimum quantity of
labour he knew was characteristic of human-
ity.   We are often reminded that money

cannot do everything. 'Perhaps not,' argued Mr. Brent, 'but it can give a good deal, and you can't tell me anything else that can give so much.' His schemes were as varied as ingenious, and, as a rule, till the inevitable explosion came, were extremely profitable both for himself and his associates. Some of them, indeed, had expiated their fraudulent proceedings by various terms of imprisonment; but Brent on these occasions invariably disappeared until the hue and cry had blown over. What his real name might be nobody knew; he had rejoiced in innumerable aliases, and William Brent was his present travelling name.

There was one thing singular about the man. His associates were generally lavish of the spoils that fell to their share. Brent was not; he made money and he kept it, and it was probably this possession of ready money which enabled him so often to escape the consequences of his wrong-doing. If he had devoted the same amount of skill and energy to any legitimate calling he would have probably been a far wealthier man. The profits may be great on illicit transactions, but there is always more or less a certain amount of blackmail to be paid by those engaged in them. 'Honour among thieves' is a very fallacious adage to place trust in, and Brent had more than once paid high to close the compromising mouth of an old associate. Gifted with great coolness and audacity, he had so far borne a charmed life, and was regarded with no little awe and veneration by his companions, over whom he ruled with great firmness and authority; but there was amongst them one to whom it was notorious that William Brent yielded a deference he accorded to no one else, and, moreover, that it was certainly not from love that he was so subservient to the ideas of this ancient comrade. Brent was a self-reliant, well-educated man, subtle in his plans, and dictatorial to those concerned with him in their accomplishment; but when old Creasey chose to assert himself—and the violent tempered old man was much given to doing so—Brent usually yielded. There were various rumours concerning his influence over him, mostly to the effect that he possessed knowledge of Brent's early life that the latter much dreaded to have published; but these were all vague and confused. Certain, however, it was that he yielded to the domineering old man in a way that he did to no one else.

This worthy was at the present moment in prison, where no small period of his life at recurring intervals had been passed.

CHAPTER VII

SARAH'S LOVE LETTER

'WELL, Mary, what do you think of him?'
inquired the banker, as he and his daughter
sat *tête-à-tête* at dinner the evening after Fred
Hallaton had left them.

'He is a nice, gentlemanly young man,'
replied the girl. 'I rather like him; but
don't you think it rather odd, papa, that he
should know Miss Mercer?'

'No, I can't say I do,' replied Mr. Lydney.
'Miss Mercer is a very good-looking young
woman, and I should think by no means difficult to know. I dare say she has a pretty

numerous acquaintance amongst the young men here.'

Mary Lydney said no more; she and Hallaton had got on very well together, but she couldn't quite get over that bow upon the Esplanade, although the subject had never been alluded to between them since.

When two or three days had passed without Fred Hallaton making his appearance at the Dragon, Sarah Mercer began to get somewhat uneasy; although she did not care for him she did not wish that this man should escape her toils. It might or it might not suit her to marry him, for Miss Mercer went so far as to picture that circumstance as sure to be at her option in due course, but it gratified her vanity to think that she had one of the officers from Exeter dangling in her train; and when three days elapsed and she

still neither saw nor heard of Hallaton, Sarah
began to have misgivings. In her experience,
and it was by no means circumscribed, she
had found that constant interviews were
necessary to maintain her thrall. When her
admirers, from either accident or design,
ceased to see her frequently they were
speedily disenchanted. The fact obtruded
itself that, free from the glamour of her
splendid and rather sensuous beauty, Miss
Mercer was a somewhat vulgar, half-educated
young woman, and her first idea had been to
treat Fred with considerable hauteur when
he should appear. He was to be thoroughly
well rated for his neglect, and then forgiven.
But unfortunately for the carrying out of this
programme, Fred's presence was necessary,
and he still shunned the Dragon. Sarah was
naturally a passionate woman, but she could

control her temper when she saw good cause for doing so. Fred Hallaton's chains were not quite so tightly riveted as she had deemed them. She changed her tactics, and despatched a short note to the delinquent.

'Why are you angry with poor me?' it ran. 'You might at least come and tell me what I've done wrong.—Ever yours, Sarah.'

Could Fred Hallaton but have seen the sullen, angry face that bent over the paper as those few words were penned, it might have saved him much future misery. Fred, indeed, on his side, was not a little wrath with the fair Sarah himself. He knew as well as Miss Lydney that the salute on the Esplanade had been given with *malice prepense*, and it angered him that Sarah had deliberately placed him in such an awkward situation.

But Fred was too deeply smitten to nurse his indignation for long. He was already once more meditating a call at the Dragon, when Sarah's note was put into his hands, and, it need scarcely be said, that effectually clinched his resolve.

He was received with much cordiality. Sarah's face flushed with downright pleasure at the success of her stratagem. She honestly was excessively glad to see him again. She had missed his adulation. It was a necessity to this girl that some man should be always pouring honeyed words into her ear. Even her father was pleased to see the young fellow again. As we know, Joe Mercer had somewhat ambitious aspirations for his daughter, and muttered to himself, ' He would do, if he'd take a fancy to her, as Sam 'ud say. Gentlemen don't come shinning round every day.'

'Now, Mr. Hallaton,' exclaimed Sarah, 'I will take you to see old Bob Mutter if you like, and you can hear from his own lips all that he has got to tell about the old inn.'

'I think I'd rather hear it from you than from him,' rejoined Fred, with an ardent glance at his enslaver. 'Let us have one more look at the old ball-room before you begin.'

Sarah laughed, and rejoined : 'Well, with you to protect me, I don't mind, but I honestly don't care about going there by myself. It gives me the creeps—but come along,' and she led the way.

On arriving at the door, she turned the handle, and then said, 'I can't open it.'

'It's a little stiff from disuse,' suggested Fred. 'Let me try.'

She stood back while he essayed to open

the door. He turned the handle sharply, and gave it a good jerk, and then remarked, 'No wonder we can't get in. It is locked.'

'I wonder what that's for,' exclaimed Sarah. 'Wait a minute, I'll go and ask father for the key.'

They accordingly wended their way back again, and found Joe Mercer and Brent talking together in the bar-parlour.

'We want to have a look at the old ballroom, father, and somebody has locked it up. Have you the key?'

Joe Mercer and Brent exchanged a rapid glance.

'Yes, but it is upstairs,' responded the former, after a short pause. 'I have locked it up because the floor is not safe.'

'Why, father,' exclaimed the girl, 'we went in there the other day. The room was

1 2

dusty and ghostly enough, but there wasn't a board even creaked under us.'

'What the devil are you doing here, sir?' suddenly inquired Brent, so fiercely that the other three looked round in utter amazement to see what had produced this explosion.

Standing in the doorway, with both ears unmistakably cocked, was Mr. Tootell. If ever a man had curiosity limned in every line of his face, if ever a man was listening to a conversation of absorbing interest, it was Mr. Tootell at that moment.

'What am I doing?' he replied, in answer to Brent's question. 'I have just dropped in for a tankard of mild ale, and to see how my old friend is. Ah! Mr. Hallaton, I hope I see you well, sir. No cause to ask after you, Miss Mercer, you look blooming.'

Miss Mercer responded by an indignant

shrug of her shoulders, while Hallaton returned the old gossip's greeting with a con-
temptuous stare.

'By the way, Joe, you never told me
about the old ball-room. I'd like to see it.
That reminds me, I've never been thoroughly
over the old house yet.'

'Well then, you can't see the old ball-room
to-day, that's all I have got to say,' replied
Mercer. 'In my mind the old ball-room is
unsafe. I've locked it up, and I'm not a-goin'
to open it for anyone. I'm not a-goin' to have
any broken legs lying about my premises.'

'Well, Mr. Mercer,' said Hallaton, laughing. 'I don't think there'll be much risk of
that, but if you don't want us to go into the
room, of course that's sufficient.'

'No, no, tut, tut!' exclaimed Tootell.
'You young gentlemen are always so hasty.

I'm very anxious to see that ball-room. I
don't mind even if there is a little danger.
To think now, Joe, that you never mentioned
that ball-room to me before.'

'I'm sorry I can't oblige you, Mr. Hallaton, but I stick to what I say. I thought it
best to lock that room up, and locked I intend
to keep it.'

'Quite right, Joe, quite right,' said Mr.
Tootell, as Sarah and her admirer quitted the
parlour. 'Not the thing to let foolish young
people like that go exploring by themselves;
but now they're gone, you and I'll just go and
have a look at that floor by ourselves. Might
be something to be made of that room, Joe,
who knows! We might get up a free and
easy there. I'm rather a card, you know, in
that way, and I'm sure I'd be always ready to
oblige.'

Brent cast a meaning look at Joe Mercer, and then left the room.

'Odd thing,' remarked Mr. Tootell, 'that man always reminds me of some one I used to know long ago.'

'Who might that be?' asked the other uneasily.

'That's just what I can't call to mind, but it's some one I knew before I came here, I fancy. It puts a man out not being able to think of a thing like this,' said Mr. Tootell meditatively. 'Now, Joe, what about that ball-room?'

'We'd best have this thing made clear at once,' said Mercer angrily. 'I keep a house of entertainment in which there are certain rooms set apart for the public; the remainder of the house I intend to keep for myself. If the public rooms ain't enough for you, you'd best go somewhere else for your liquor.'

'No, no, Joe,' replied Tootell. 'I'm not a-goin' to desert an old friend like that; but it's impossible for me to advise you without looking over the premises, you know.'

'Advise me!' cried Joe, 'what about? Who the dickens asked your advice?'

'Now don't get hasty,' replied Mr. Tootell; 'of course I thought you were asking my opinion about doing the house up a bit.'

'Then you had best understand,' retorted the landlord of the Dragon, 'that I don't want your opinion about that or anything else;' with which sweeping disclaimer of any assistance Mercer left his guest to finish his ale by himself.

The idea of a sort of Bluebeard's cupboard in the Dragon roused Mr. Tootell's

curiosity to a feverish height. He felt that
he must see the inside of this locked room.
What reason had Mercer for keeping it shut
up? That its being unsafe was a mere excuse
was palpable, and while he drank his ale Mr.
Tootell's busy brain was lost in vain conjecture
as to what might be the secret of this carefully guarded chamber, and how he was to
obtain a peep into it. He had not lived in
Exmouth all these years without having heard
of the ball-room and the ancient glories of the
Dragon, but it had never occurred to him till
that morning that the ball-room was still in
existence. He knew that a considerable part
of the house was shut up, but had never
before felt the slightest curiosity about these
empty unfurnished rooms. But now there was
a mystery about them, he felt he should never
rest till it was solved. He wondered whether

it was possible to get a peep in at the windows of the mystic chamber. The Dragon was built like a T, of which the top faced the road while the tail ran back into the garden, and on which the windows of the ball-room opened. Mr. Tootell knew enough of the house to know that this tail of the T was the disused part, and that of course in that was the room into which he was so anxious to penetrate.

Mr. Tootell finished his ale, and was about to take his way home again, when he suddenly bethought him that it was worth while to take a turn round the garden and see what he could make out at the back of the house. It was a large old-fashioned garden by no means carefully kept, and in which there had never been the slightest attempt to conform to the modern fashion of groups of small beds in intricate patterns, with trim narrow borders of lobelia, golden chain, or other similar plants. The large grass-plot in the centre was surrounded by various shrubberies with great deep borders in front of them, in which the flowers grew in wild luxuriance and looked almost as if they had been sown broadcast. It was evidently but very roughly cared for, and even Tootell could see that in the hands of anyone who had a real love for a garden it had great capabilities. Prying about and making diligent use of his eyes, Mr. Tootell had little trouble in making out to his own satisfaction which were the windows of the ball-room. Those three tall windows, of which the centre one ran down to the ground, and was flanked on each side by a bay-window stopping just short enough of the walk outside to allow for a seat in each, pointed unmistakably to the object of Mr. Tootell's quest, but it required only a glance to see that they were boarded up on the inside, and that therefore, as he reflected ruefully, there was no opportunity for making a peephole unless the glass was first broken. Mr. Tootell's further researches were suddenly stopped short by a significant cough, and it was beautiful to see then how absorbed he at once became in the cabbage roses, the view, or anything else indeed except the old ball-room.

'What!' said Brent, as he advanced with a mocking smile on his lips, 'as you couldn't see the inside you thought you would come and look at the out. Well, that's it, and now I hope you're satisfied.'

'Very interesting indeed,' replied Mr. Tootell; 'I can quite fancy it being a most excellent room for the purpose. Dancing inside, then people stepped out by the window

and doubtless had refreshments of all kinds.
I tell you what,' continued Mr. Tootell, 'if
the landlord in those days knew his business
he had lots of little tables and chairs all over
that grass-plot.'

'And if the landlord of these knew his
business, he would allow no prying old fools
about his premises;' with which far from flat-
tering observation Mr. Brent turned sharply
on his heel and made his way round to the
front of the house, where the landlord of
the Dragon stood, his hands thrust deep into
his pockets, and apparently buried in deep
thought.

'It's devilish unlucky, Mercer, that that
inquisitive old idiot should have overheard
your daughter ask for the key of the ball-room.
By the way, I told you the other day somebody had been in there.'

'Why, what's the matter now?' inquired Joe.

'He's gone pottering round to the garden to have a look at the house on that side; he has made out the ball-room, and he'll never rest till he gets a peep at it.'

'Well,' said Joe, with a chuckle, 'if as much as he can see through the windows will content him, he is welcome. I saw to the boarding up of those windows myself, and I'm blessed if there's a chink to put an eye to. No, no, he'll do us no harm that way, and I'll take good care he never has the key. But I'll tell you one thing that looks queer; he says you remind him of some one he met long ago.'

'No, did he say that?' inquired Brent eagerly.

'Yes; says he can't recollect who, but

thinks it was some one he knew before he ever came to Exmouth.'

Brent drew a breath of relief. ' Then it's all right,' he exclaimed; ' but, of course, I might have known it was, he never did know me in Exmouth. I had left it before he came here.'

As Mr. Tootell walked back to the town again he muttered, ' That Mr. Brent is so rude ; it's extraordinary I do not recollect him.'

But Tootell was used to such rebuffs, and was often wont to remark to himself, with a sigh, ' There ain't no politeness left in this world.'

CHAPTER VIII

THE WARNING

THE weeks slipped by. Exmouth had never been gayer than it was that summer. Garden parties, tennis tournaments, cricket matches, water picnics and dances followed each other in rapid succession. Plenty was also going on in Exeter, and the revels in both places were attended by the people of each town. Fred Hallaton threw himself into the fun going on round him with all the life and vigour that characterised his nature. In the ball-room, in front of the nets, or in front of the wickets he threw himself into the pastime of the hour, heart and soul. He was by no means a bad fellow, but he was apt to pursue the pleasure of the moment without counting the cost, and at the present time was playing a game that has often brought infinite tribulation to the player. He was paying marked attention to one woman, while he was madly in love with another.

Mary Lydney was no foolish, sentimental young woman, to let her heart go out of her keeping at the first few courtesies that a man might pay to her. She had had two disappointments, the latter of which she had born with becoming resignation, but the first had been a very different matter. Her heartstrings had been sore wrung about that first love affair; for a long time she had not known how it was that her betrothed had suddenly left her. But persistent questioning forced from her father the humiliating fact that her *fiancé* had

broken off his engagement because he could
come to no satisfactory arrangement in money
matters with Mr. Lydney. What particular
point he had taken umbrage at she had never
cared to inquire. She felt sure that her father
would be most liberal in his offer of settle-
ments, and she flushed with indignation when
she thought that this man, who had professed
to love her so dearly, had loved not herself
but her money. As her father's only daughter
she supposed that some of these days she
should not only be very well off, but that her
father would make her a handsome allowance
if he approved of her choice, and she thought
that the man whose requirements in this
respect her father had failed to satisfy, must
be indeed greedy of gold. She liked Hallaton,
and could not help being aware that he paid
her marked attention, but she was not likely to

let her heart go lightly out of her own keeping
again. Then, moreover, she knew of his
acquaintance with 'that very objectionable
Miss Mercer,' and she often wondered whether
he saw anything of that young lady now.
She had never asked him; they had tacitly
agreed that that fair damsel was never to be
the subject of their discourse.

Strangely enough, Sarah was equally
curious to know if Fred saw much of Miss
Lydney, but Hallaton sternly repressed all
inquiries in that direction, and imperious as
the girl was, and great as was her power over
him, she found her lover, too, had a temper
of his own, and, strange to say, she liked him
all the better for it. Sarah Mercer had been
so accustomed to rule her swains right royally
that it interested her to have a man at her
feet whom she could not quite deal with as

she pleased. That society generally had noticed how attentive the young artilleryman was to Mary Lydney it is needless to say, and also that society waggled its head and whispered that all was arranged between Mr. Hallaton and the banker's daughter. Some of those dear elderly ladies to whom a past scandal is a thing preserved, but never buried, whispered ominously that the thing had happened twice before, that Mary had no difficulty in getting engaged, but in her case that never seemed to lead to a wedding.

As for Dicky Chives, when the rumour first met his ears, he put down his pipe, and said gravely, and in awe-struck tones, 'Is this true, you fellows? I don't go gadding about, you know; but has he gone too far to be saved, because if he hasn't I'll speak to him!'

But his comrades generally replied that Hallaton was making uncommon strong running if he didn't mean it, and that if he was not engaged yet he was as good as. On hearing which Dicky resumed his *brûle-gueule*, puffed a heavy cloud of smoke from under his moustache, and grimly ejaculated, 'There's another good man gone wrong!'

Dicky consequently never said anything to Fred concerning this rumour. He hated to see his chums marry, because he knew that they then became lost to him in that capacity. It was not that the better halves of some of these lost sheep had not striven to make their houses pleasant to their husbands' old friend, the difficulty was with Dicky himself; he got on very well with ladies once induced to mingle with them, and indeed would have been rather a favourite

with them if he could only have been persuaded
to go more frequently amongst them, but, to
use his own expression, he 'shied at a petti-
coat.' It must have been, I suppose, the
mental strain required for the making of
small talk, for he was a man to whom,
except in the matter of tobacco, a lady's
presence imposed no very unaccustomed
restraint. If Chives had asked Fred whether
he was going to marry Miss Lydney, that
gentleman would probably have told Dicky
not to be a fool. 'I visit a good deal at
their house at Exmouth; it's all rot to think
just because a man is a little civil to the
daughter of the house that he is thinking
about marrying her,' and at the present
moment it was probable that Fred had never
taken thought to himself of what would be
the end of either of his love affairs.

Yet with all the gaiety he was mixed up in, Hallaton found time somehow to pay many a visit to the old Dragon Inn. He made a flimsy pretext of a passion for hearing these smuggling legends, and had even been taken by Sarah to see old Bob Mutter. He had made that veteran happy by a largesse of silver and tobacco, and endured, as he laughingly remarked, two or three stupendous lies from the lips of that drunken old sailor. But, for the most part, he sought his information from Miss Mercer's own pretty mouth, to which his own at times got in closer proximity than strict etiquette warranted.

'I can't think,' said Sarah, as she walked lovingly with Fred Hallaton in the garden one autumn afternoon, 'what father's fad is about that old ball-room. He keeps it most jealously locked ; as for its being unsafe, that's all moonshine.'

'It doesn't much matter,' replied Hallaton. 'It is only an old man's whim, I fancy. It may be that your father has got it into his head that some of the lumber and old furniture we saw there is valuable.'

'I sleep a good way from it,' replied Sarah, 'but sometimes I hear strange noises that sound as if they came from the old room. I told mother so the other day, and remarked that if the ghosts of the old smugglers had come back, they must have come in very substantial form ! '

' And what did Mrs. Mercer say ? '

' Nearly snapped my nose off,' replied the girl laughing. ' Told me I was old enough to know better, and that she would trouble me to hold my tongue, and not go talking about such things, adding, "If you go gabbling about ghosts I shall have the girls afraid to move about the house now the days are drawing in." Father and Mr. Brent, too, are quite touchy about any allusion to that room.'

'I can't see what Mr. Brent has to do with it,' said Hallaton, ' any more than I can see what on earth he is doing here. By the way, what does he do here?'

'I'm sure I don't know,' replied Sarah; ' he goes out very little, and never, to my knowledge, into Exmouth. He seems to spend most of his time talking to father.'

Hallaton here turned the conversation into more personal channels. His question had been asked from very idleness, for what Mr. Brent's business might be at the Dragon was a thing in which he felt no interest.

Inside the bar parlour it was evident that something unusual had occurred to disturb the usually tranquil conversation that went on between Joe Mercer and his guest.

'This letter is serious,' exclaimed Brent. 'That inquisitive, chattering magpie Tootell was bad enough, but even if he did succeed in recollecting me, although it would be awkward, still there could be no such consequences as would happen in this case.'

'Read the letter again,' replied Mercer sententiously.

'Letter,' returned the other; 'it's only a line from one of my most trusted confederates, a man who has been in a good many big things with me. He don't say much, but Jim can say a good deal in a few words. There's nothing more than this—"Mind yourselves; Creasey is out." And if he had said the Devil is unchained I shouldn't have considered it more serious.'

'Well, I can't quite understand it,' said Mercer. 'To begin with, who is Creasey, and what is he out of?'

'Out of prison, curse him! Creasey is the bane of my existence, the millstone that has been round my neck all my life. But for Creasey,' continued Brent passionately, 'I might have been something very different. I've never stooped to be the mere vulgar bandit that Creasey is—a man who has adopted burglary as his calling.'

Carried away by his own tempestuous feelings, Brent did not notice his companion's countenance, but suddenly his eye fell upon Joe's awe-struck face, and pausing, he said with a laugh, 'Do I frighten you, old man?'

'I knew nothing about Creasey,' was the reply; 'you never told me you were mixed up with people of that sort, and what is the use of calling things by such ugly names? I don't hold with robbery, mind you.'

'Ah, you don't,' said Brent, 'pray what do you call our present business?'

'Well, it is smart trading, if you must talk about it,' said Joe. 'I get all the produce I can off the farm, and sell it at the best market.'

Brent burst into a fit of laughter. 'Now,' continued Joe, 'what about Creasey? Not that I've any desire to make his acquaintance, but how can he interfere with us? Does he know you're here?'

'No; but he will,' rejoined Brent. 'As I tell you, there's no shaking him off. He'd find me if I was in the midst of the

Australian bush. He always does, except
he's locked up.'

'Well, what does he want, when he has
found you?'

'Money,' said the other; 'but that's not
the worst of it. He'll want to know what
I'm doing, and, worse still, to have a hand
in it.'

'Oh, Lord,' said Joe, 'and then I suppose
that he'll blow the gaff.'

'No; to do Creasey justice, he's not that
sort quite, but he is just as bad. Out of his
own business he's the stupidest chap I know.
Give him a centre-bit, a jemmy, a pair of
goloshes, and a box of safety matches, and I
believe he is clever, but for anything that
requires headwork and combination he is a
hopeless dunderhead. He has spoilt three or
four of the best things I ever planned; not

that he has " rounded " intentionally ; he has let the cat out of the bag from sheer stupidity.'

' But can't you give him money and beg him to go away for the present ? '

' You don't know him,' said Brent. ' The obstinate old man claims to have a great liking for me. Go! Not he. He'd settle down close to us, break into a house once a week just to keep his hand in, and finally " crack " the Dragon some night, just to see what " his dear boy," as he calls me, is about.'

' Then what do you propose to do ? ' said Joe. ' I told you the other day I wished I'd never gone on with it. I should have liked to back out of it even then ; but now that we are making money so fast I own I should like to risk it a little longer.'

'What we must do is this,' replied Brent.
'As soon as Creasey makes his appearance—
and appear he will, as sure as fate, though at
present he neither knows my address nor the
name I'm going under—we must stop the
concern, and I must make a clean bolt of it
abroad.'

'Why abroad?' inquired Joe Mercer.

'Simply because that's the only place
where I've a chance of shaking off Creasey.
Foreign towns confuse him, and, moreover, the
foreign police are lynx-eyed. Creasey is
never long on the Continent before he dis-
appears into retirement.'

'And then?' said Mercer

'It'll be time to think what then when
I've shaken off my incubus,' and with these
words Brent suddenly vanished down the
passage in the direction of the ball-room.

Joe Mercer had most clearly expressed his feelings in his conversation with Brent. He had been very loth to go into a business which he knew placed him within the trammels of the law. Hard bargains he had driven, and very close to the wind had he sailed again and again in his dealings ; some of his doings could by no means morally be condoned, although legally no man could interfere with him. At first he had sternly declined this affair as too risky, but Brent was a plausible man, and painted in glowing terms the enormous profits he had made by the same scheme two years before. 'It burst up suddenly,' concluded Brent, 'and we all had to quit and travel at short notice, but we made a pile of money at the game while it lasted.'

This story oft repeated into Joe's avid

ears, added to the suggestion that the old
Dragon Inn was the very place for their
purpose, and on offer at a very low rent,
at last induced Mercer to embark on the
speculation. For once his greed for gold
got the better of his habitual prudence, and
the landlord of the Dragon found himself the
possessor of a thriving business, but a
business which brooked no investigation.

CHAPTER IX

DICKY'S EYES ARE OPENED

ALTHOUGH Mr. Chives had no taste for balls and picnics, and regarded lawn tennis with tolerant contempt, yet he was a most energetic man concerning all matters of sport, and always running about the country to play cricket, to shoot, fish, or to perhaps ride a horse at some local meeting. Nothing came amiss to Dicky of this kind, and even rat-catching met with favour in his eyes. These manifold pursuits brought Chivy, as he was often called by his intimates, in contact with a large and varied circle, and wherever he was quartered the number of gentlemen of all degrees who called at the barracks to see him was the cause of much chaff among his brother officers.

His servant was constantly pursuing him with 'Gentleman, please, to see you, sir,' and whether the gentleman was interested in rats or politics, whether he was member for the borough or the landlord of a sporting tavern, who had simply called in to give Dicky 'the office' that there would be parlour field sports at his little place, was generally an open question. Let him be stationed where he would, Mr. Chives and his brace of terriers, which their proprietor proudly boasted would face any living thing, were sure speedily to be well-known figures in the town. Fuss and Fidget were a couple of broken-haired terriers, quite as restless as their master, and con tributed not a little to his notoriety. They apparently believed their sole mission on earth was the destruction of vermin, and that they were taken out walking for no other purpose.. A mistaken idea on their part that the killing of cats was laudable had more than once got Mr. Chives into hot water. What had brought that ubiquitous gentleman over to Exmouth this fine autumn day is of no moment, but seven o'clock saw him sitting down to what threatened to be a solitary dinner at the Beacon, when suddenly, to his great delight, a tall, florid, stalwart man entered the coffee-room, and, after greeting him warmly, volunteered to join him in his meal.

Doctor Nicholls was a man much of Dicky's own kidney, and they had met many times and in many places in pursuit of their favourite pastimes. How Nicholls had acquired the sobriquet of 'The Doctor,' to which his position as a veterinary surgeon by no means entitled him, I don't know, but as such he was well known for many a mile round Exmouth. 'The Doctor' was a busy man, but contrived to combine business with pleasure by dint of untiring energy. He was here, there, and everywhere, and there was little that went on either in the town or about it but what came to his ears. Not that he was given to gossip—far from it. His talk was chiefly of dogs and horses, and such scandal as escaped his lips was chiefly equine.

'Well, Mr. Chives, how goes it?' he exclaimed, as he took his seat opposite him. 'Having settled over the Leger, it's getting time to lose more money in trying to pick the winners of the two big back-end handicaps. Have you got a fancy?'

'No. I spotted the winner of the Cesarewitch five years ago, and lose a few pounds every year in endeavouring to do it again.'

'We must try and do better for you this time. D'ye know Sam Mercer?'

'No; never heard of him. Who's he? inquired Chives.

'Never heard of him? Well, that's queer, too, considering Mr. Hallaton's a great pal of yours. However, no matter; Sam's a great pal of mine, and is as clever a man as there is in the ring. He generally gives me a hint worth following towards the finish of the piece, and if he don't, why then it's not good enough to touch. What's the news at the barracks? Fuss and Fidget been in mischief lately? Any old woman's best mouser missing?'

'No,' rejoined Chives, 'the "quads" are all right ; the mischief's amongst the bipeds. Fred Hallaton's gone wrong.'

'Why, what's the matter?' asked the doctor, with no little astonishment.

'He's going to be married,' replied Dicky, so solemnly that the last dread formula of a sentence to death might have been expected to follow. 'However, it's a good thing for him, I suppose. Miss Lydney will have a pot of money, I'm told.'

'Very likely,' rejoined the doctor ; 'but that won't matter to Mr. Hallaton.'

'Oh, won't it, rather. You don't suppose a subaltern of Horse Artillery is a millionaire, do you?'

'No ; but your chum's not going to marry Miss Lydney—at least, I'll lay liberal odds against it.'

'Why, everyone's talking of it, I'm told,' said Chives. 'It's as good as given out. The banns are up, so to speak.'

'Yes; I know all about that, but what about the other? Why, Mr. Hallaton's always out at the Dragon. Her brother's a great friend of mine, but I've no liking for Sarah Mercer, and the man who takes her for better or worse may make up his mind to do with the latter.'

'What the deuce are you talking about, and who on earth are these Mercers?' inquired Chives.

'Why, you saw that handsome girl Hallaton was walking about with when you played at Exmouth, that was Sarah Mercer; her father keeps the old Dragon Inn just outside the town.'

'And you think Fred's after her,' said

Chives, much surprised at this double complication.

'Don't know what he goes out to that tumbledown place for if he isn't,' replied the doctor, 'but he'd better be careful; he's playing with a tiger-cat when he's fooling with Sarah Mercer.'

Mr. Chives had much respect for the doctor's opinion. A man of his knowledge concerning horses and dogs he thought must be an equally good judge of womankind, and he came rapidly to the conclusion that Fred Hallaton was in a fair way to make an egregious ass of himself. This young misogynist, however, knew his hot-headed chum too well to think that he could do any good by interfering.

'If Hallaton must marry,' he remarked at length, 'I suppose Miss Lydney would be a good match for him, though why a fellow can't let well alone I can't think.'

'Yes, I should think so,' observed the doctor, ' and if you mean would it be better than running away with Sarah Mercer— infinitely. Lydney was born to, and has always held, a high position in the place, and, judging by appearances, is well off.'

' And no near relations, bar his daughter, to leave his money to,' remarked Chives, suddenly developing mercenary propensities.

' About having no near kith and kin, I wouldn't be so sure,' rejoined the doctor. ' Lydney undoubtedly had a younger brother, who disappeared abruptly from Exmouth under a cloud. I don't know exactly what it was, for I was only a boy at the time. He has never been seen or heard of in the place since. But then, again, he has never been said to have died. If anything happened to the banker, I shouldn't be surprised to see him turn up again.'

'Ah! and you think he might share in Miss Lydney's inheritance?'

'Oh, I'm sure I don't know,' replied the doctor laughing, 'but hang it, that's enough of this. If we are to go in for speculation, let's talk over the weights of the Cesarewitch.'

'It's getting time I was off,' said Chives, as he took a cigar from his case and rose from the table.

'Ah, going back to Exeter, I suppose. I'll walk down to the station with you. I want to persuade you to come with me to Newmarket next week.'

'If I can get away,' replied Chives, 'I don't mind if I do. You are going for the whole week, I suppose?'

'No ; business won't allow of that. We'll run up from here on the Monday, have Tuesday and Wednesday at Newmarket, and be back here again on the Thursday.'

'Write it down, old man,' said Chives. 'If the chief 'll let me, I'm on,' and with that he disappeared into the train.

'A good sort that,' mused the doctor as he walked slowly away. 'I'm glad I told him what I did at dinner. If ever a young man wanted a word in season, it's Hallaton just now. I don't know whether he's a man who'll bear talking to, but I should think if anyone could warn him that he is in a fair way to make a fool of himself it's Chives. They're great allies, and Chives is a little the elder of the two. However, I've done all I can, and it's no particular business of mine after all,' and with this the doctor dismissed

the subject from his mind and betook himself
to his own abode.

The object of all this solicitude was, however, not one whit disturbed about his doings
or their results. He had spent the afternoon,
with great satisfaction to himself, at the
Dragon, where he had pursued his flirtation
with the fair Sarah more hotly than ever.
He had dined at mess, and was now playing a
rubber with apparently no care on his mind
save the winning of the odd trick, and yet for
all that he had found two or three disagreeable letters upon his table on his return from
Exmouth : one from his bankers, calling attention to the fact that his account was considerably overdrawn. He had not been racing
since Goodwood, but it is by no means necessary to attend races in order to bet upon
them, and the ill-luck Fred had experienced

at Goodwood had stuck to him ever since. He had struck one of those veins of ill-luck familiar to all who gamble ; he could do nothing right. Even when it really did look as if fortune was within his grasp his fancy at the eleventh hour succumbed to the exigencies of training. On two occasions also did he encounter that bitterest of misfortunes known to the backer of horses—his selections won, but were disqualified, the one for foul riding, in the other case for the omission of a penalty. Then there was a jeweller's bill, which also astonished him not a little, as bills of that nature are wont to do.

He was not given to jewellery himself, but Miss Mercer had developed a very pretty taste that way, and Fred was one of those careless young men who scarcely note the cost of a bangle or such-like knick-knacks. 'Well,

he had said to himself as he dressed for mess, ' I
suppose luck will turn some day. However,
at present there's nothing for it but to have
another dig into capital. I must sell some
more of those railway shares. I can buy in
again, at a slight difference no doubt, when I
make a *coup*.'

Alas! that *coup* so seldom comes; and if it
does we very rarely buy in again!

Fred Hallaton played a pretty good rubber
at whist; he had a liking for cards, and had
assiduously cultivated all games thereat in
which skill tells, but though a fair performer,
he had one fatal weakness—he never adhered
steadfastly to the same points. The consequence was, after a very successful run at the
conventional garrison points, he would probably experience just the reverse when playing at his London club for very much higher

stakes.   To-night he was holding great cards,
and had just triumphantly called 'Three by
cards and two by honours; out, treble, double,
and the rub,' as Chives entered the room.

'Halloa, Dick!' he exclaimed; 'what
wickedness have you been up to all day?'

'I've been over to Exmouth,' replied
Chives.   'Never you mind what about.
Perhaps I was buying a horse; perhaps I was
trying a dog; and then, again, perhaps I
wasn't.'

'And perhaps you don't want to tell, and
perhaps we don't want to know,' retorted
Hallaton laughing.   'Still, if I was so downright ashamed of myself, I'd fudge up some
excuse to cover my misdeeds.'

'Ah,' replied Chives, 'my wickedness
hasn't been very great.   I shouldn't wonder
if it brings its own punishment all the same.

I dined at the Beacon with Dr. Nicholls, and I've agreed to go with him to Newmarket if I can get away. I suppose Thornton,' he continued, turning to the adjutant, 'there won't be any trouble about that for four days?'

'I should think not. We'll see about it to-morrow.'

'Going to Newmarket, are you?' said Hallaton. 'I've a great mind to come too.'

'You'd better put that idea on one side,' said Thornton. 'I'm sure the chief won't let you both go.'

'Rather a bore that,' returned Hallaton. 'And Dicky has got decidedly first call. I say, Chivey, when you go over to your quarters I'll go with you.'

'All right,' replied the other, 'I'm going there now,' and the pair left the room together.

'Now,' said Hallaton, 'as I can't go to New-market, I shall want you to do something for me. I've been having an awful bad time lately. It set in a hailstorm at Goodwood, and it has been blowing great guns ever since. I can't turn a trick, and I'm a terrible lot out in the last three months.'

'Give it up man,' replied Chives, 'it is no use persistently following your bad luck.'

'You're quite right, but I've a chance now, Dicky, to get a bit back, I think. I got a line to-night from the cleverest tout I know, and he tells me that Sugar Cane will about win the Cesarewitch.'

'Of course I'll back her for you,' said Chives, 'but answer me one question. Why don't you back her yourself.'

'For the best of all possible reasons ; I'm warned not to do so till the day. This man tells me that the mare belongs to a very queer party, and if they can't get their own money on satisfactorily, she'll not run at all. Her performances are not very great, but he tells me I needn't take any notice of that. She is a very much better mare than she is credited with being, and has got wonderfully well in.'

' Well,' said Chives, who had been turning over the pages of a turf guide, ' her performances are not very gaudy, certainly.'

' No, but for all that the public have been nibbling at her, at forty to one. If her number goes up put me a hundred on her.'

' I say, that's a lot of money to knock down ; don't you think a pony will do ? '

' Not a bit of use,' replied the other ; ' if I don't land a good stake I must sell out shares of some kind or another ; a hundred won't make any difference while I'm about it.'

M 2

'All right, old man, I'll do it, though I won't promise to follow your tip, nor I am afraid will you take warning by mine. Now, Fred, I heard all about your visits to the old Dragon Inn to-day. Don't be angry with me, and don't ask who my informant is, but this is what I was told. You'd better play with a tiger cat than make love to Miss Mercer.'

'Nicholls—for I suppose he was your informant—was d——d impertinent to comment on my actions. It was like his confounded impudence to pry into my private affairs,' said Hallaton hotly.

'That'll do; no need to flare up,' rejoined Chives. 'I've said my say, and you'll hear never another word from me about Miss Mercer. Now, let's talk racing.'

CHAPTER X

THE SWEETS OF THE SUGAR CANE

MR. CHIVES having obtained his leave started
as agreed on the Monday with the doctor, and
duly arrived at Newmarket, if too late for the
day's racing, still in excellent time for dinner.
Chives was very fond of a bit of racing when
it came in his way, entering with the keenest
zest into the sport of the thing; but his speculations were on a modest scale, and not wont
to occasion him much anxiety when they
proved unsuccessful. He usually put as many
five-pound notes as he could conveniently lay
hands on into his breast pocket, and, in his

own vernacular, when he had 'punted' them all away he stopped. It was not his first visit to the metropolis of the Turf, but for all that he was not learned in Newmarket. As for the doctor, he was an old *habitué*. He had been a race-goer for upwards of thirty years, and was well versed in all the intricacies of the running ground, whether Across the Flat, the Rowley Mile or the Cesarewitch Course, &c. He knew them all. Dinner over, he proposed that they should stroll down to the rooms and see what was doing. Plenty of speculation was going on there about the big race on the following day, and Chives and the doctor looked on much amused at the stirring scene before them.

Suddenly Chives was startled by the cry of 'What'll anybody lay me against Sugar Cane?' He turned sharply to the direction from which the voice proceeded, and saw a quietly dressed man, who was leaning upon a crutch-handled stick.

'Here's forty hundreds Sugar Cane,' was the quick response. The first speaker simply nodded as he took out his betting book, and then observed laconically, as he pencilled the bet, 'I'll do it again.'

'Here's thirty to one Sugar Cane,' roared another speculator.

'Done in hundreds,' quietly remarked the man with the crutch stick. 'Monkeys if you like.'

'No, thank you, Mr. Roach,' replied the professional who had laid the last bet.

Inquiries after Sugar Cane became now pretty numerous. It was obvious that several backers had followed the inspiration of Mr. Roach, and the price against the mare shortened rapidly.

' By Jove,' thought Chives, ' for once I do believe Fred really has got hold of a good thing. Sugar Cane looks like becoming a hot favourite,' he observed, turning to the doctor.

' Don't know anything about her,' replied that worthy. ' So little indeed that I forget whether she's ever run ; but the confederacy to which she belongs are dead sharps, and that man Roach, who " put her up," and backed her to-night, very often does commissions for that stable. However, I've had about enough of this, and feel a bit tired after the day's travelling ; besides everyone at Newmarket gets up early.'

So the two strolled out of the rooms and made their way leisurely up the High Street in the direction of their lodgings. They were lounging along, when suddenly from a narrow by-street on their left came a half-stifled cry of 'help!' Both men turned sharply round, and the doctor suddenly exclaimed, 'Come on, Chives. By God, there's a pack of roughs have got a man down, and are robbing him.'

In the centre of the narrow street one man was kneeling on another while his three companions were endeavouring to rifle the pockets of their victim, who, though unable any longer to cry for assistance, from the fierce grip on his throat, still struggled manfully with his assailants. The doctor dashed in boldly at the robbers, but these latter were by no means disposed to let their prey escape them. Pausing in their work of plunder, three of them fiercely confronted the new comers, and with awful maledictions bade them go about their business.

The doctor might not possess much science, but he was a powerful man for his years, and grit to the back-bone. He was not to be cowed by curses, and went boldly in at the foremost of his antagonists. But in Dicky Chives he had a most valuable ally. Though low in stature, Dicky was broad in shoulder, rather bull necked, and in chest like a Highland bull. He not only possessed great strength, but was an exceptionally good man with his hands; and his quiet 'All right, doctor, wire in, I can lick a couple of such trash as this in no time,' struck no little awe to the hearts of the two ruffians who were confronting him. The observation too, was followed up by some half-dozen blows straight from the shoulder, which, as the doctor laughingly remarked after the fray was over, resembled the kicks of a horse more than the application of man's natural weapons.

Like all ruffians of this sort, the robbers

were arrant curs at bottom, with little stomach for hard fighting. The battle was of short duration, two or three minutes, and the gang took to their heels, and as the attacked man struggled breathless to his feet, the doctor exclaimed, 'Sam Mercer, by all that's fortunate! We would have been glad to do anyone such a turn, of course, but I'm real glad Sam, we were in time to pull you out of the fire.'

'Reckon you're right, doctor,' gasped Mercer; 'the tarnation skunks had pretty near fixed me. Ugh! ugh!' he continued, still choking a bit. 'If I had only been up in time to have one kick at that bushwhacker who was hanging on to my windpipe!'

'Sure you're none the worse?' inquired the doctor.

'Nary worse,' replied Sam; 'the thieves

only took my wind. I managed to hang on
to the flimsies. Haven't the pleasure of
knowing you, sir,' continued Sam, turning to
Chives ; ' but I'm awfully grateful for your
assistance. Guess we've got to have a drink
over this as soon as possible ; ' and with that
the bookmaker led the way up the High Street.

Sam Mercer's lodgings were no very
great distance from their own, but the doctor
declined Sam's proffered hospitality, said it
was getting late, and they would all be the
better for a good night's rest.

' Don't you be afraid about the drinks, old
man ; we'll find time to wash our mouths out
with you to-morrow—at Jarvis's, perhaps,
when we've got the Seizerwitch off our minds.
Good-night.' And with hearty hand-grips
the three men separated.

.   .   .   .   .

A grand October day, when the crisp air
seems to act like wine on the system—one of
those bright clear days when, if striding
through the turnips with the first crackle of
frost on them, one feels all over like ' killing,'
or if on Newmarket Heath like backing
winners—a day that seems to augur success
to whatever we have undertaken; but on a
race-course there are always gathered the two
opposing armies, and the battle must go
against one side, be it the backers or the
fielders. The small preliminary race that
precedes the *cheval de bataille* of the second
October week has just been run, and is
followed by the slight lull which takes place
before the hoisting of the numbers for the
Cesarewitch. Standing against the rails of
Tattersall's ring are two men who have apparently met for the first time that day.

'Well, Sam,' said the bookmaker, who had laid Mr. Roach the odds against Sugar Cane the previous night, 'I'm glad to see you looking all yourself. It was all over the town this morning that you'd been rushed by a lot of rowdies on your way home from the rooms, and robbed, and half murdered.'

'Not quite so bad as that,' rejoined Mercer, 'but that was about the programme, if a friend of mine had not stepped in and spoilt it. But you had no end of a game on at the rooms after I left, hadn't you, over Sugar Cane? What's it all mean?'

'Well,' replied the other; 'it beats me. I *did* think I knew something about that one, and when Crutch Roach first put her up I thought it was only to make a market, and laid him forty hundreds, but I soon found it was a genuine commission. He often does them for that stable, you know. Bless your soul, before half an hour was over, people were tumbling over one another to get on the good thing. The mare looked like becoming a red-hot favourite, when just as the rush was at its height Captain Figg quietly exclaimed, "Here's ten thousand to a thousand Sugar Cane or any part of it." We all stared, for you know what Figg is; when he begins to lay 'em in that way they're as good as dead ; but perhaps the most puzzled man of the whole lot was Crutch Roach. He evidently couldn't understand it. However, he shot the captain for ten monkeys, and then the duel began in earnest, but the captain never flinched; he tired out Roach and all Sugar Cane's other supporters, and finally drove her back to twenty-five to one—no takers.'

'It's a queer start,' said Sam, 'and a question of who knows most. Neither of 'em make many mistakes, nor are likely to have bet as they did without direct information. However, here go the numbers,' and Sam commenced ticking them off on his race-card. 'Sugar Cane goes, at all events, and there's pretty certain to be a move either for or against her now,' and so saying, Sam Mercer plunged into the throng in the exercise of his calling.

He had been for some minutes vociferating the odds, booking bets, and holding mysterious confabulation with his brethren, when he was suddenly touched upon the shoulder, and on turning round found himself confronted by Dicky Chives.

'What can I do for you, sir,' inquired Sam.

'What price Sugar Cane?' inquired Dicky.

'They are taking twenty to one,' replied
Mercer.

'All right, I've a commission to back her.
Will you lay me twenties?'

'Certainly, Mr. Chives. What shall I put
it down to? Ten pounds or more?'

'I want to back her for a hundred,' replied Dicky.

Mercer hesitated for a minute or so, as if
thinking, and then said, 'You're not backing
it for yourself, sir?'

'Certainly not,' replied Chives, 'I never
bet in such sums as that.'

'Very good,' said Sam, 'then I'll lay you
two thousand to a hundred,' and having pencilled the bet the bookmaker again started off
on his vociferous career.

'Well,' thought Chives, as he walked
away to seek some place from which to see

the race run, 'I don't know whether Mr. Mercer doubts my stability, but it struck me he was rather unwilling to bet with me.' But in this he did Sam a great injustice. Sam Mercer was not the man to forget what a good turn Chives had done him the night before. He did not know positively, but from what he had seen during the last few minutes, he had come to the conclusion that there was something not right with Sugar Cane. A bookmaker cannot afford to indulge in sentiment, but had not Chives so clearly said he was backing the mare for somebody else, Mercer would have strongly advised him to leave it alone. He could not have explained what it was all about, but he had been far too long in his profession not to understand the signs of the market. Crutch Roach was silent to-day, and it was evident that the backers of Sugar Cane were chiefly composed of the general public, while, ominous sign, Captain Figg and three or four of the most astute operators in the ring seemed to have endless money to bet against the mare.

However, the roar of the bookmakers is hushed at last, and the cry from the stand proclaims 'they're off.' Chives, who has regained the fly which he and the doctor have chartered for the day, stands up on the seat, and adjusts his race-glasses. As the horses pass through the gap, Chives descries the green and white hoops of the mare well in the van. 'Sugar Cane is going well,' he observed quietly to the doctor.

'Why you haven't backed that one, surely,' exclaimed Nicholls.

'Not for myself, but I have for Hallaton.'

'Much?' inquired the doctor, laconically.

'A hundred,' replied Chives, with equal brevity.

'Money thrown away,' replied his companion; 'I'll tell you all about it afterwards. It's as rascally a business as that precious confederacy ever indulged in.'

With the details of the race we have nothing to do. The running of the only horse which bears upon this history—Sugar Cane—may be briefly described. After lying in front for about three-quarters of a mile, she dropped unaccountably in the rear, and some distance from home her jockey ceased to persevere with her, and she finished quite at the tail of the ruck.

'Sorry for Fred,' muttered Mr. Chives, as he closed his glasses. 'I'm afraid from what he said that he is rather in a hole about money matters, and this afternoon's work isn't calcu-

lated to improve things,' and then it struck
Dicky Chives as rather singular that Hallaton's
hundred had gone into the pocket of Sarah
Mercer's brother. Of course it made no
difference whether he took the odds about
Sugar Cane from Sam Mercer or any other
bookmaker, the result would have been the
same, but if the doctor was at all right in his
estimate of the young lady, the Mercer family
seemed destined to be very unfortunate acquaintances for Fred Hallaton.

'Now doctor,' he said at length, 'tell me
what you heard about the mare before she
started.'

'That she was likely to run pretty much
as she did. It seems that Gregory, one of the
two confederates, had a trial while Carver, the
other, was away from home, and that the mare
failed to accomplish what she was asked. In

his anxiety to save the money for which he had backed her he gave Captain Figg a heavy laying commission, without saying a word to Crutch Roach, who was backing it for the stable, and who, he was dreadfully afraid, would begin by saving his own money before he began looking after that of his employers. This all leaked out about an hour ago, and I'm told that there will be a very pretty row between Messrs. Roach, Gregory, and Carver to wind up with. Well, I hope we shall do better over the Middle Park Plate to-morrow, for I've had a bad race over the Cesarewitch.'

'Yes, and besides Hallaton's money there's a modest tenner which has been reft from the house of Chives, and which must if possible be recovered to-morrow.'

CHAPTER XI

WAS IT A WIG?

ALTHOUGH Mr. Tootell was thick-skinned, still he had his feelings. It took, no doubt, a good deal to get down to them, but they were there, although they might not lie near the surface, and the more Mr. Tootell pondered on it, the more confirmed he was in his opinion that he had been treated with scant courtesy on his last visit to the Dragon. He determined to abstain from visiting that hostelry, and in his self-conceit thought that this would be a severe deprivation for Joe Mercer.

'I'm sorry for Joe,' he muttered to himself; 'he'll miss my daily budget of news sadly, but when it comes to calling people " inquisitive idiots," it's coming it rather too strong. It's time such language was at once pronounced unparliamentary, and that is where Joe failed. He allowed such language to pass without taking any notice of it. No; I'm sorry, but I must give Joe up. One can't frequent a house which contains a Blue-beard chamber, and where you're called an inquisitive idiot for wanting to know what's in it.'

But if Mr. Tootell deemed that he was punishing the landlord of the Dragon he was inflicting agonies on himself. What there might be or what went on in that mysterious ballroom haunted his mind day and night; he pictured to himself the most preposterous

scenes by turns. Sometimes the skeleton in
the cupboard was a veritable one, then his
imagination depicted that the room was full
of treasures, that old Joe had in some
mysterious way discovered that there was a
walled-up cellar which contained all kinds of
laces, velvets, wine, etc., a buried legacy from
the smugglers who had haunted the house in
days of yore. Yes, that would account for
Joe Mercer's taking the Dragon. He had
somehow discovered the secret that all these
valuable goods were contained within its
walls, and was now busy moving them
surreptitiously away, so that his landlord
might not lay claim to what was clearly more
his property than anyone else's. In short,
there was no end to the romances which Mr.
Tootell built up for himself about the Dragon
and the locked-up ballroom. Three days had

elapsed and then the old talemonger could stand it no longer; he felt that he really must go out and see how things were going with the Mercers. If he could not solve the mystery of the Dragon, he could at all events keep an eye upon that little flirtation of young Hallaton's. He was taking two or three turns on the esplanade preparatory to starting for the country, when his attention was attracted by a grey-haired old gentleman who was slowly sauntering up and down the sea wall. That he had never seen the old gentleman before was quite enough for Tootell: Who was he? And what was he doing in Exmouth? were two questions that a strange face invariably aroused in his mind.

The grey-haired gentleman had apparently plenty of time on his hands. He sauntered along in most indolent fashion, and constantly paused to admire the view and inhale great gulps of the strong seabreeze. Presently he seated himself on one of the benches, and to one of Mr. Tootell's inquiring mind this was an opportunity not to be resisted. Taking a seat beside the stranger he ventured the remark that it was a lovely morning.

'Yes,' was the reply, 'it's years since I saw it last, but Exmouth is still what I have always remembered it, a sweetly pretty place.'

'Ah! knew it of old, did you, now?' said Mr. Tootell. 'Now what might be your idea, sir, of *years*?'

'Thirty odd; time enough to have made great changes in the place, as no doubt it has in the people.'

'Ah! that was before I came here. I suppose you had a large acquaintance when you were here before?'

'Not very,' replied the stranger; 'I was only here a short time. Are Lydney and Sons, the bankers, still to the fore?'

'There have been no sons in the house,' replied Mr. Tootell, 'since I've been in Exmouth. It's Lydney and Daughter, although they don't write it on their cheque-books. Did you happen to know them, Mr. ——? Johnson I think you said your name was.'

The stranger smiled as he bent his head. 'I was acquainted with one of them. By the way, there was a famous inn in these parts in those days. I don't suppose it exists now, probably been pulled down to make way for a fashionable hotel.'

'Not a bit of it,' rejoined Tootell. 'The Beacon—of course, you mean the Beacon — is as flourishing as ever. Bless

you, I ought to know, I was in the "public"
line myself, once; kept the White Stag here
for years.'

'No,' said the stranger quietly, as soon as
it was possible to interrupt the other's
loquacity; 'the inn I mean stood about a mile
outside Exmouth. It was a celebrated house;
I can't recollect the name.'

'Not the Dragon,' exclaimed Mr. Tootell,
his eyes very nearly starting out of
his head with excitement. 'It wasn't the
Dragon, Mr. Johnson, was it?'

'That's it,' replied the stranger; 'the
Dragon.'

'Why that has been taken by an old
friend of my own, old Joe Mercer; but he
isn't doing much good with it; he won't
be guided by me, or else he would start a
little gathering there every week, call it the

"Sons of Harmony," or some such name. It would be attractive, and draw custom. People like a little music with their liquids, leastways that's my experience. Got the very room for it, and all. You recollect the old ballroom there?'

'Can't say I do,' replied the stranger. 'I only stayed there for two or three nights, and recollect very little about the place.'

'Ah! then I've no doubt you would like to see it. I'm going out there now. If you like to walk out with me, I'll ask old Joe to show it us.'

'You're very good,' replied the stranger, rising, 'and some other time I shall be very proud. Just now I must go back to my lodgings. Good morning, sir.'

'Good morning,' replied Tootell. 'Don't forget to give my old friend Joe a turn. It's a nice walk, and you get a good glass of ale at the end of it. A good fellow is old Joe, but obstinate, damned obstinate.'

'Now,' said Mr. Tootell to himself, as the stranger walked away, 'I do wonder who he is. Very suspicious, the way he behaved about his name. Never said honestly his name was Johnson. And what on earth could he have wanted at the Dragon Inn all those years ago?' A misty speculation that could only have occurred to a man of Tootell's insatiable curiosity. However, he regarded this as a still further reason for delaying his visit to the Mercers no longer—he was disappointed that he had failed to persuade the stranger to accompany him. In his cunning, Mr. Tootell had thought of making a cat's paw of his new acquaintance, and instigating him to ask for a sight of the mysterious chamber. That being out of the question, he must now trust solely to his own efforts.

On arrival at the Dragon, somewhat to his dismay, Mr. Tootell found himself received by Mrs. Mercer. She and Brent were engaged in an animated conversation, and there was evidently considerable difference between them. At the sight of Tootell their tongues at once stopped, and Mrs. Mercer greeted him with a somewhat uncourteous 'Good morning.' As for Brent he took no notice of the visitor, but smoked on in solemn silence. To a man like Tootell this was irritating past endurance. He was a man to whom 'talk' was a necessity, and conversation from his point of view, usually took the form of asking questions. Mrs. Mercer speedily left the parlour, while the exasperating brevity of

Brent's replies to the interrogatories Mr. Tootell put to him were in that gentleman's opinion simply sickening. As he said afterwards, the fellow *wouldn't* know anything. Again the thought flashed across Tootell that the man's face was not altogether strange to him, and then all at once a new idea struck him. It was capitally done, and was calculated almost to defy scrutiny, but was this man Brent wearing his own hair? Was it a wig or was it not? Mr. Tootell, bear it in mind, from his histrionic tastes had considerable knowledge of making up for the stage, and after staring intently at Brent for some minutes arrived at the conclusion that it was a wig. In spite of the contempt he usually manifested for him, Tootell's prolonged scrutiny seemed to make Brent uncomfortable.

Rising from his chair he exclaimed with

forced jocularity, 'If you want to stare at me, old gentleman, I expect you to pay for it.' With that he strolled out of the parlour, leaving Tootell more impressed than ever with the idea that he (Brent) was wearing a wig, and much perplexed as to by what stratagem the said wig was to be got off its wearer's head. Clear up these two points he felt he must; a peep into Bluebeard's chamber he must have; and to see what manner of man was disguised under that wig was likewise necessary to his happiness; but how to compass either of these things he was completely nonplussed.

At this juncture Joe Mercer entered the parlour, and he welcomed Tootell in more kindly fashion than the others had done.

'Well, Joe,' said Mr. Tootell, 'I've come

over to have a little chat with you. I've been thinking over that little scheme of ours —a little harmony once a week, you know. Suppose we go and have a look at the room?'

'Now, once for all, understand that room's locked, and it ain't agoin' to be unlocked. I can manage my own business without any assistance from you.'

'Well, well, I'm sure I don't want to interfere, but they do say——'

'Who's they?' interrupted Joe, sharply.

'Oh, I don't know exactly. People will talk, you know. However, never mind, Joe, I've got a new customer for you. I met a nice old gentleman on the Esplanade this morning who knew Exmouth years ago. He asked particularly after the old Dragon Inn. I told him all about it, and said he'd get as good a glass of stingo here as anywhere about Exmouth.'

' Did he ask for me by name? '

' No, Joe, he did not, and that's the truth. His own name was Johnson, that is, he didn't say it wasn't. He is probably come to stay some time in these parts. I daresay he would be more comfortable with you than where he is. I'll see about it for you.'

'Don't you trouble yourself,' rejoined Mercer. ' We don't care about any more boarders. The Missis don't care about having so much cooking going on.'

' That Brent seems to stick to you. By the way, you haven't found out what he's doing down here,' remarked Mr. Tootell confidentially.

' Never mind about Brent,' replied Mercer. ' What about this stranger who inquired for the Dragon? What aged man was he?

'About your own age. It's singular he should recollect anything about the Dragon. Why, you can't remember it in its famous days, can you, Joe?'

'No; I've heard of 'em. But they were over before my time. Nobody, I reckon, remembers them except old Bob Mutter.'

'It is odd, now you mention it, that a stranger to Exmouth should ever have known of the old Dragon Inn,' remarked Tootell. 'I must ask him how it came about the next time I see him,' and, seeing no further chance of clearing up either of the two mysteries which disturbed him, the old gossip rose to depart, resolved to make diligent pursuit of this fresh hare that had crossed his path.

On Brent's return to the room Mercer

told him Tootell's story, remarking that it was certainly rather singular that a stranger's main recollection of Exmouth should be the old Dragon Inn.

For a few minutes Brent sat musing. 'Yes,' he replied at last, 'I can't understand that. I can't cipher it out. From the description I shouldn't be much surprised if the stranger is Creasey. How that man always contrives to find me out I can't tell, but he does. I should not have thought that he had ever even heard of the Dragon, nor am I even aware that he knows anything about this part of the country. At times I think he knows my real name, but he has never said so, positively.'

'I don't suppose it is Creasey,' replied the other. 'That Tootell always makes a great fuss about anyone until he finds out who he is.' Blessed if I don't think he is always afraid of over-looking an Emperor in disguise.'

'It's all very well,' said Brent, 'to think I am skeary about Creasey, but I should like to have a look at this stranger, without his seeing me. As I told you the other day, if it is Creasey, it's all up with our business, he will insist upon joining in it, and bring us to grief, as he always does; he is too unlucky, not to say too careless a confederate to trust in any game, add to which he is so terribly well known. Why, they have got his photograph in every prison and leading police station in England.'

'Yes,' said Mercer, decisively, 'if that fellow has found you out we must give it up. I've never run such a risk before, and I never will again.'

'And you never made so much money before.'

'No,' replied Joe, 'and if we can carry on for a twelvemonth more, and get out scot-free, I'll not say it hasn't been worth running.'

'We must keep a sharp look-out,' rejoined Brent, 'and as a precaution I must endeavour to have a look at this stranger.'

In pursuance of this resolve Mr. William Brent relaxed from his usual habit of avoiding Exmouth, and commenced taking an occasional constitutional on the Esplanade. At war with the laws of his country as he had been from his youth up, he considered that he owed his immunity from chastisement in great measure to the strict concealment of his identity; whatever the nefarious scheme he might be engaged in, he invariably adopted a disguise of some sort, and he was

famous among his confederates for his
dexterity in making up. The victims of his
frauds would have often been dumbfounded
if they could have seen the real man in place
of the cleverly disguised swindler who had
outwitted them. The good fortune that had
so far attended him was perhaps making him
too daring in his schemes, but his audacity
never occasioned him to neglect the slightest
precaution nor to run unnecessary risk. He
did not like Mr. Tootell's visits to the Dragon,
but he could not see how to prevent them.

For the first time it had struck him that
morning that Mr. Tootell had suspected his
disguise ; in such tortuous paths as he was
accustomed to tread a quick eye and a good
memory for faces were essential, and he not
only recognised Tootell, but had recalled to
mind where he had met him. He did not

want Tootell to recognise him, but reflected that if it came to the worst Mr. Tootell could allege nothing against him beyond that he used to frequent the tavern in London of which he, Tootell, was then the proprietor, in company with men of rather dubious character.

CHAPTER XII

'TAKE ME WITH YOU'

'I SUPPOSE we shall lose you now very soon, Mr. Hallaton,' observed Miss Lydney, as she paced by his side up and down the Esplanade. 'You officers always go away about this time.'

'Yes, I'm off in a week or so, and I'm sorry for it; but one must be attentive to one's relations, you know; and I rejoice in an uncle who is a perfect martinet upon that point. He was in the service himself, so that he knows perfectly well the time at which long leave commences. I shall have to spend a month with Sir Robert in Kent. However, there's one thing, the fun here is pretty nearly over ; but what a jolly season it has been, has it not ? '

' Very,' replied Mary ; 'but that's rather a selfish remark on your part. The fun is over, and you're going away. Have you no sympathy for us who are left behind ? '

' You can't think I shall forget the many friends I've made here, and least of all Miss Lydney.'

' Oh, I don't know about that ! ' replied the young lady, laughing. 'I daresay you'll have forgotten all about us long before you come back.'

' You can't think that of me,' rejoined Hallaton. ' You know I couldn't if I would.'

' I think you're talking great nonsense,' replied Mary. ' If rumour may be trusted, you'll perhaps not forget one person here, but that is neither me nor any lady of my acquaintance.'

'I don't understand you,' stammered Fred, but his face too clearly showed that he did, although he had never dreamt that his constant visits to the Dragon had of late become quite common gossip in Exmouth. That, as one whom it to some extent concerned, the rumour should be slow to reach Miss Lydney's ears was only natural, but it had at length, and she had heard it with no little indignation. She felt that it was likely to be true, and she was very angry that Fred Hallaton should have dared to put such an affront upon her. His attention to her had been most decidedly marked, and that he should presume under those circumstances to carry on a low intrigue with a girl like Sarah Mercer was a positive insult. She felt the more indignant on discovering that the liking she had always had for him had ripened into something warmer; if she was not in love with him, she was drifting into something very like it, and this intelligence opened her eyes to the fact. Her first impulse was to take care never to see him again, but she was a proud sensitive girl, and on consideration thought it would excite less remark if she broke off their intimacy by degrees. She was aware that he was going away before long, and that would facilitate their lapsing into a distant acquaintance. She would probably never have opened her lips to him on the subject had he refrained from love-making on this their last walk, for although Fred Hallaton did not know it, Mary had determined if possible it should be that.

There was silence between them for two or three minutes. Fred Hallaton was not often taken aback, but for once he had nothing to say. Miss Lydney was the first to speak.

'I am not,' she remarked, 'given to credit all the idle gossip that comes to my ears, but on this occasion I can vouch that you do know this young woman, and it is somewhat to my astonishment that you find her attractive. Of course your intimacies I have no wish to comment on, but to talk sentiment to me, when you are notoriously paying your attentions to another woman and *such* a woman, is simply an insult.'

'But believe me——' began Hallaton.

'*You*,' she interrupted contemptuously; then suddenly recovering herself, 'It's getting cold, she continued, 'and I shall go in. I'll not trouble you any further, Mr. Hallaton, we'll part here,' and with a haughty bow Mary Lydney dismissed him.

As Fred Hallaton walked back towards the railway station, he reflected ruefully, as many of us have often done, that he was in for a bad time. The world was running askew with him just now, and when that is the case it makes it no better that the broth is of our own brewing. Men who gamble cannot be always successful, and the old adage ' It's well to be off with the old love before you are on with the new,' is doubtless the result of bitter experience.

'Serve me right,' he muttered. ' Hang it all. I just feel as pitiful a cur as ever crawled. By Jove! she was far too good a girl to treat in that fashion. How she did flash out. Who could have dreamt of pretty Mary Lydney's eyes lightening like that? Who could have told her about Sarah?'

Because the Dragon was little frequented and that by a class inferior to his own, Fred

Hallaton fell into the mistake of supposing
that his visits there escaped observation. It
was not likely. He forgot that Sarah had
often accompanied him back to the outskirts
of the town, and though he might not have
been seen on the Esplanade with her, plenty
of Exmouth people had seen them walking
together. That Sarah Mercer was carrying
on with one of the young officers from Exeter,
and giving herself more airs than ever in
consequence, was the subject of much talk
amongst her old friends and acquaintances.
Mr. Tootell also was not the man to refrain
from commenting freely on what he saw at
the Dragon, so that one way and the other
Fred Hallaton's affair with Sarah Mercer was
quite as much discussed amongst the middle
class people of Exmouth as his flirtation with
Miss Lydney was amongst those of his own

station. Mary was not given to gossiping with servants, but she had been quite unable to stop her own maid's loquacity when that young person first became aware of Mr. Hallaton's iniquities.

Fred began at last to think he had made a precious muddle of his affairs generally. Did he want to marry Miss Lydney? No, he was not clear about that. She was a sweet girl, by whose side it was very pleasant to saunter through a summer afternoon, but marriage was another thing, and yet he knew he had given her to suppose he had that end in view. But if he did not want to marry her, still less did he wish to quarrel with her, and he knew that henceforth he could expect nothing but the coldest salutation from Miss Lydney, nor was it likely that he would ever make his peace with her again. Sarah Mercer was superbly

handsome, but then he certainly did not con-
template making her his wife, and he did not
quite see how that flirtation would end. Once
or twice he had resolved to see her no more,
but his infatuation was too strong and again
and again he returned to drink of the Circean
draught. Do not believe that a man cannot
be for a little while in love with two women
at the same time. Hallaton was genuinely in
love both with Mary Lydney and Joe Mercer's
daughter, but his love for the first was of a
higher order than that which he had conceived
for the latter. Had Sarah Mercer not crossed
his path it is quite possible he might by this
have resolved to win the banker's daughter, if
he had not already done so; but Sarah
intoxicated him, and as she gave him every
encouragement, he had not the strength of
mind to break her thrall.

'It's well,' he muttered to himself as the train bore him along the line to Exeter, 'that I am going on leave. My affairs seem in a devil of a mess all round. Miss Lydney has taken things into her own hands and dismissed me. Whatever chance I might have had of winning her I have lost by my own folly ; as for Sarah, 1 am half sorry I ever saw her, I'll wish her good-bye and have done with it, and when I come back from leave make a stern resolve not to cross the threshold of the Dragon. I'm rather foolish even to say " good-bye," I believe, but I can't help it. I must see her once more. Then I'm rather in a scrape about money matters. There's another hundred gone over that brute Sugar Cane. Dipping into capital is a very good game while it lasts, but the worst of it is, it don't last long. Let's see, this is Wednesday, and Chives has

wired for one day's extra leave, and so won't
be back till Friday. I have no doubt they
will give me leave to go that day without
waiting for his appearance. Dick is always
true to time. I'll go and bid Sarah good-
bye to-morrow, and be off by the evening
mail next day.'

By the time Hallaton had arranged his
programme to his entire satisfaction, the train
had reached the station, and Fred made the
best of his way to the Barracks.

He had made no mystery of his approach-
ing departure. There was no reason he should ;
most of his friends—just as Miss Lydney did
—knew that he was going away in a few days
on two months' leave, but there was one place
in which Fred had instinctively felt that it
would be better not to mention it, and that
was at the Dragon. He felt it was likely to

be productive of a scene if Sarah should discover that he was going to part from her for so long, and yet there was something too pitiful in sneaking away without avowing it ; and as he took his way into Exmouth the next morning, he had quite determined that he would bid Sarah farewell and explain to her that it was best they should say good-bye to one another for good.   But though he was unaware of it, the news had already reached Miss Mercer's ears, and though ignorant of the precise day she did know that her lover was going to leave Exeter for a time, and Miss Mercer was very determined that something definite should be settled between them before he went.   She felt tolerably sure that he would not go away without seeing her, but she was beginning to feel extremely uneasy about it when Fred made his appearance.

The girl advanced to meet him, all radiant with smiles, and Hallaton thought he had never seen her look handsomer than she appeared that morning, as, clad in her close-fitting dark serge dress, which showed off the superb figure to perfection, she stood in the porch of the old inn awaiting him.

'I began to think that you had clean forgotten me,' she exclaimed, with a pretence of a pout, as she adjusted the gay cherry ribbon at her throat. 'I haven't seen you for three whole days, and now I hear that you're about to leave Exeter.'

'Only for a time,' he replied, as he drew her towards him and kissed her.

'Ah, you men,' she said, as she gently disengaged herself from his embrace. 'You call it only for a time, and you're away months; don't you know that days are months when one loves, and you have taught me to do that, Fred.'

Hallaton winced; he felt guiltily conscious that he had been making desperate love to this girl almost from the day he first met her; no doubt she had been willing enough to meet him halfway, but it did flash across Fred that she was doing a good deal more than that now, and that this 'good-bye' would be difficult to say, more especially if, steadfast to his resolution, he persisted in making it final. It is not so easy to tell a passionate, sensuous young woman, who has just answered your kiss with a frank confession of her love, that you have come to say farewell, and break off all relations with her. One thing was clear to him, namely, that the porch was rather too public for so tender an interview as this promised to be.

'Come round to the garden,' he said. 'I want to have a long talk with you.'

They took their way to the large garden, which ran round the ball-room at the back of the house, and where they had paced up and down many an afternoon during the past summer.

'I have been in a fever,' said Sarah, ' ever since I first heard you were going away. I thought you were never coming again. Ah, I did you injustice; I might have known you would never leave me like that.'

'I'm going away,' he said, ' a little sooner than I expected, but how came you to know I was going at all?'

'That wretched old Tootell told me,' replied the girl with an angry flash of her eyes, ' and the spiteful old thing quite giggled when he did so. He hates me as much as I

hate him.   He only told me to make me mad,
and he did.'

'What did you say to him, Sarah?'

'Oh, never mind what I said to him; he
won't like me any the better for it, but tell
me about yourself first.   How long are you
going away for?'

'About two months,' he rejoined

'Two months, and I am not to see you
for two whole months—two long months!
Oh, Fred, if you cared half as much about me
as you pretend to do, you could never bear to
leave me for all that time.'   She was not really
in love with him, in spite of all the passion she
was displaying, but he did please her fancy,
and it flattered her vanity to have a gentleman
at her feet.   She had made up her mind to
marry him if she could, and she did not like
the idea of parting from him for so long.

'It can't be helped,' he replied soothingly. 'I have relations whom I am bound to go and see occasionally.'

'But you will write, write constantly, won't you?'

'Yes, my darling,' replied Fred, once more caressing her.

It was weak; he knew it was. If he were determined to put an end to this affair, to open a correspondence with her was the most imprudent thing he could do.

A glow of conscious triumph filled her heart, and she felt that this man was given into her hands. They walked up and down for some time exchanging those many nothings that enter into the composition of all love-making. Every art that she possessed the practised coquette exerted to win him. She was tender and passionate by turns, and

Hallaton, intoxicated by her charms, felt his resolutions melting like wax, and when the time came to say good-bye, he felt it was impossible to tell her that he looked upon their parting as final.

'When do you go?' she murmured, as the last words were exchanged between them. 'I shall see you once more, shan't I?'

'No, dear, this is good-bye. I go by the night mail to-morrow night.'

'Take me with you,' she cried, as she threw her arms round his neck. 'I can't bear it; I can't live without you,' and, his resolutions scattered to the winds in the delirium of the moment, Fred Hallaton consented.

CHAPTER XIII

'SOONER OR LATER SHE'LL MARRY HIM'

IF Mr. Brent had for reasons of his own commenced to take his exercise on the Esplanade at Exmouth, yet he did it in a fashion peculiar to himself. He did not pace up and down that fashionable promenade after the manner of its habitués, but generally slunk along on the side of the carriage way farthest removed from the sea, but for all that his restless eyes took note of all the passers-by that strolled up and down the causeway. The fourth morning he espied Mr. Tootell in close conversation with another man, and this he had a shrewd suspicion was the object of his

search. This probably was that old gentleman of whom Tootell had spoken, and whom
Brent suspected of being his bugbear Creasey.
Many of us are afflicted with our Old Man of
the Sea, that terrible friend or relation whom
it is impossible to shake off; and it is grati-
fying to think that the criminal classes are no
more exempt from this infliction than their
neighbours. He was too far off to be perfectly sure whether it was Creasey or not,
although he felt quite sure about Tootell:
and yet to approach nearer would be dangerous. And should Tootell catch sight of him,
that garrulous old gentleman would be sure
to salute him and so call his companion's
attention to it. Brent was most decidedly
anxious to see if this was Creasey, but he was
equally desirous to keep Creasey in ignorance
of his own presence. Brent was a man of

resource. Dogging the couple at a considerable distance, he kept them in view till he ran
across what he wanted.

One has not to go far to seek a man with
a telescope by the seaside at any watering-
place, and as soon as he encountered one,
Brent borrowed his glass, and in two minutes
had ascertained that his suspicions were well-
founded. Tootell and his companion had
turned towards Brent. Another steady stare
through the telescope, and he handed the
glass back to its owner. It was Creasey ; and
Brent, as he hurried away, felt no doubt in
his mind that Creasey had come down to
Exmouth in search of him.

'It's wonderful,' he muttered to himself,
'how impossible it is to shake off that old
man. I left, as I believed, no clue behind me
when I came down here on this business, and

here he is again, not only on my trail, but very close to the end of it. It would be absurd to suppose that now he has got hold of that talkative old fool he will be more than a day or two in discovering me.'

Brent, as we shall see later on, was to some extent mistaken. He was perfectly right about its being Creasey, but he was wrong in thinking that illustrious malefactor's business in Exmouth was to discover him. Mr. Creasey had come down there on some private business of his own, though should he stumble across Brent he ould doubtless desire to dip into his purse as in days of yore.

Brent made the best of his way back to the Dragon, and at once communicated to Joe Mercer his discovery.

'It's no use, Mercer,' he said, 'I shall have

to be off. Of course it don't matter for a day
or two ; it would take him some little time to
find out our game, but it will be only a
matter of time ; we shall never keep him out
of the house. It's a great pity just as we're
coining money at it to have to give it up.
There's only one thing, Creasey knows nothing of you ; don't you think you could
manage to run the thing alone—that is,
without me ?'

'I don't know,' replied Joe, 'but I do
know that I'm not going to try. It's a pity,
for as you say we're doing well at it, but it's
too risky.'

Then ensued a long discussion between
the two men, and finally it was arranged that
their nefarious vocation should still go on, at
all events until Mr. Creasey appeared at the
Dragon. In short, although they had not

confided in one another, the Mercer family were all prepared to decamp without beat of drum. Little was seen of Fred Hallaton by his brother officers the day after what was to have been that final interview with Sarah. He was busy, indeed, making all his preparations for what he practically knew might prove a very lengthened absence indeed. In the madness of his passion he had promised Sarah to take her away with him, and what the end of that was to be was a thing he rather shrank from contemplating. He had settled to travel by the night mail to town and had arranged with Sarah that she was to meet him at Exeter Station. He thought it would be prudent not to dine at mess, for fear that some of his brother officers might volunteer to accompany him to the station, and he was certainly not anxious to advertise

the fact of his having a *compagnon de voyage*
to all Exeter. He would have something to
eat quietly at the Rougemont, and then kill
the time as best he could until the train
started.

In his anxiety to leave Exeter without
attracting attention Fred Hallaton had resolved to start a few hours before his leave
actually commenced. He confided his inten-
tions to no one, and therefore his brother
officers, if they did trouble their heads about
it, would not imagine that he would start till
the next morning. Now, it so happened that
there was a train down from London which
reached Exeter just ten minutes before the
train he proposed to travel by left that
city. Had he dined at mess he would have
known that Dicky Chives was expected back
at that time, and that consequently it was

very probable that he would run across him at the station. Things had mended very much with that gentleman on the Wednesday at Newmarket; he had backed several winners, the sport had been generally good, and he confided to the doctor that he had thoroughly enjoyed himself, to which that gentleman drily responded, 'Winning in fine weather on a racecourse is about the most exhilarating thing that I know of.' It was the morning of their final day at Newmarket, and seeing Sam Mercer in front of the rooms, Chives went up to him, saying, 'I don't belong to Tattersall's, and therefore always settle on the racecourse. I owe you a hundred pounds over the Cesarewitch. As I told you, I wasn't backing Sugar Cane for myself, but you won't mind taking my friend's cheque I hope.'

'Not at all, sir,' said Sam, 'that'll be right enough I've no doubt.' As he looked at it he suddenly ejaculated, 'Mr. Hallaton! It was for him you backed the mare then?'

'Yes,' rejoined Chives, 'do you know him?'

'Oh, yes,' replied Mercer, 'I've done business with him. We had a bet or two together at Goodwood. He don't seem in luck's way. I suppose you mean to see the week out, sir?'

'No,' replied Chives; 'I'm off to-day.'

'Good-bye then,' said the bookmaker; 'I daresay we shall meet again. I owe you a good turn, Mr. Chives, and if ever I can pay it, I will, you bet.'

'Well,' was the laughing reply, 'I think you might have told me that Sugar Cane was no good the other day.'

'Look here, sir,' said Sam Mercer earnestly; 'I asked you particularly if it was for yourself, didn't I?'

'You did,' said Chives.

'Very good; you can't expect me to look after all the babbies there are about on a racecourse. Besides, these infants ain't so innocent always. They often know quite as much as we do, and a bit over; all betting resolves itself into a case of who knows most. Guess I'd like to shake hands with you if you're not too proud. You're *white right through* and no mistake.'

Chives smiled as he shook hands, although perhaps Sam Mercer's final compliment he hardly comprehended, and shortly afterwards was making the best of his way back to the west country.

As the train rushed merrily through the

night air on its way to Exeter Chives fell to
thinking a good deal about Fred Hallaton ;
that he was very much embarrassed about
money matters he knew. They were bad
enough, but it is possible to be involved in
considerably worse troubles than those.
Fred had an uncle who, if he chose, could
give him very substantial help in that way.

' It's a deuced good thing he's going away,
it's the only thing that will save him, if I may
rely on the doctor's story, from a hopeless
entanglement with Sarah Mercer. If he
marries her—well, a marriage of that sort
always produces an awful row amongst all
your relations, besides everybody will know
the whole story—they'll be tabooed everywhere they go. Sam Mercer is, no doubt, a
very good sort of man in his way, but he'd be
a little awkward as a brother-in-law,' and

then turning round, he confided the subject of his meditation to his friend the doctor. The latter listened patiently, and then sat silent for some minutes.

'You want to know what I think about it,' he said at last. 'That's soon told. I know Sarah Mercer a little, but I know a great deal more about her. She has an imperious, domineering temper, but she can be very fascinating to most men when she chooses. My idea is that unless she chooses, he'll never get rid of her, and that sooner or later she'll marry him, whether she goes off with him first or not. If you think you can interfere with any advantage you had better do so, but my experience of interference in such cases is that it generally does more harm than good ; and now, I'm going to sleep.'

No further conversation passed between

the pair till they reached Exeter. Having secured their portmanteaux, they were making their way out when Chives suddenly exclaimed, as a tall young lady hurried past them in the direction of the bridge which leads to the up platform, 'What a good-looking girl!'

'She is very handsome. You don't mean to say you didn't recognise her?'

'Well, I ought to recollect her, but don't,' replied Dicky.

'Why that's the young woman we've been talking about. That is Sarah Mercer,' and the two men paused for a moment to look after her.

'It's very odd,' observed the doctor. 'What the devil can she want over on the up platform? She ought to be travelling back to Exmouth with me. However, she's an

independent young woman, and her vagaries
are nothing to me. And now I'll say good-
bye, you're off to barracks, of course.'

'Yes. Good-bye, old man,' replied
Chives; 'it's been a very pleasant outing,
hasn't it?' and with that Dicky jumped into
a cab and was driven rapidly homewards.

Having put his traps in his quarters, he
walked across to Hallaton's, but there was no
answer to his knock, and no light in the
room.

'I shall find him over at the mess, I
suppose,' and so saying, Mr. Chives betook
himself across to that establishment in pursuit, to use his own expression, of ' a bite and
a sup.' However, when he reached it,
although there were plenty of men therein
assembled, yet the man he was looking for
was not amongst them. After shaking hands

and satisfying his hunger, Chives asked what
had become of Hallaton.

'Can't tell you. I'm sure he didn't dine
at mess, and nobody has seen him all the
afternoon.'

'Spending his last night over at Exmouth,
perhaps,' said one of the others. 'He goes
on leave to-morrow, Dicky, you know.'

'If that's Hallaton you're talking of,' said
a young fellow who had just entered the
room, 'he has gone on leave to-night.'

'How do you know?' inquired Chives;
'and now I look at you, you've the air of
having been at nefarious games yourself.'

'Never mind what I've been about,
Dicky,' replied the other, laughing, 'but I
happened to be in the Exeter Station a short
time ago, and saw Hallaton come in, and he
and his portmanteau crossed to the up plat-

form. He seemed rather in a hurry, just wished me good-bye, and said he was off.'

No more was said about Fred Hallaton that evening. Nor to anyone but Dicky Chives did his mysterious departure offer any suggestion ; but knowing all he did, Chives could not help thinking that Sarah Mercer and Hallaton both seeking the same train that evening, was something more than a coincidence. That Miss Mercer should be starting by herself on a midnight journey, to begin with, was singular. A girl in her position would scarcely choose a night train to travel by, and that particular train stopped, as he knew, only at Taunton and Bristol till it reached Swindon, and would not reach even the first of those places till close upon midnight. If Miss Mercer was going on a visit to any of her friends, they must either keep

abnormal hours, or the young lady was
selecting a very inopportune hour to arrive.

Mr. Chives in the privacy of his own
quarters, as he smoked a final pipe before
turning in, summed up the case thus :—' He's
done it, has Fred, no doubt. I'm not going
to babble like a young hound before I'm sure,
but I'm afraid the story will be all over the
place before a couple of days are over our
heads, and that he will have been duly dis-
inherited, excommunicated, and all the rest of
it by an exasperated uncle within the month.
Poor Fred, he's gone a regular mucker, and
no mistake. A bookmaker in your family
may be an advantage, but not when you're so
bad at picking winners as he is, poor chap.'

CHAPTER XIV

TOOTELL IS MISSING

THE news of Sarah Mercer's elopement was by no means noised abroad so rapidly as Dicky Chives had anticipated. To begin with, nobody had actually seen them go off together, and the only person who was in possession of facts to draw that inference was Chives. The doctor was not given to talk, and though he had wondered what Miss Mercer was leaving Exeter for at that time of night, yet he did not know that Hallaton was travelling by the same train, and in short had troubled his head very little about it. Sarah was so well known in Exmouth that her absence would be certain to provoke comment ere long. But as yet it had not attracted the attention even of Mr. Tootell, avid as that inveterate gossip-monger was in news of all sorts. Still it need hardly be said that this was not the state of things at the Dragon. Her not coming home the first night her parents thought, though unusual, might be explained. She had many friends in Exmouth, and had occasionally stayed the night with them, but when she did not appear the next day, Mrs. Mercer lifted up her voice and spoke out, and when the good lady did that there was not much peace and quietness for those beneath her roof.

'She has gone off with that young Hallaton,' exclaimed the angry dame, 'the shameless hussy! She is never content without some man dangling at her apron strings, and now she has brought her eggs to a pretty market. And as for you,' she continued, fiercely turning on her husband, 'you were pretty nearly as bad as she in the whole business, dinning into her head that she ought to marry a gentleman. Gentleman, indeed! They *don't marry* the likes of her. She has gone off with him, but she'll never have. marriage lines to show for it. I warned her a score of times what the end of her gadding about and sweethearting would be, and now it has come. Well, she must go her own way. She never crosses doorstep of mine again.'

Very rarely had Joe Mercer been seen angry, but it was in righteous wrath that he rose from his chair now and brought his fist down heavily on the table.

'Woman,' he cried, 'have you no heart

for your own flesh and blood? I told her
she was fit to marry a gentleman ; so she is.
There's not a girl in Exmouth can hold a
candle to her. Ah! and she'll have a bit
more brass, too, than most of 'em. If that
Hallaton chap has tricked her he shall pay
dearly for it, as sure as there's a sun in
Heaven.' Mrs. Mercer was somewhat cowed
by her husband's unexpected wrath, but, for
all that, her household had a lively time of it
for the remainder of the day. Sarah and her
mother had never hit it off together. They
had both violent tempers, and the quarrels
between them had been bitter and frequent ;
but Joe Mercer was undoubtedly both fond
and proud of his daughter, and counted her
a fit wife for any man in the kingdom. Both
he and his wife might be held blameless as far
as they were concerned. In the first place

Sarah was utterly beyond their control, and in the second place she was no young girl in her teens, but a young woman in her twenty-fifth year, and, like her brother Sam, they deemed her well able to take care of herself, and this opinion would probably have been endorsed by all those who knew Sarah Mercer best.

No sooner was that young lady's disappearance placed beyond doubt than the news of it rapidly reached Exmouth. It may be remembered that the Hebe who presided at the Dragon bar returned every evening to Exmouth to sleep, and this was a delightful bit of local scandal to take home to the bosom of her family; all the more so because Miss Mercer had been wont to snub her and treat her otherwise with some contumely. Mr. Tootell heard the news with no little disappointment, though, as he told his in-

formant, 'It's only what I expected. I said
weeks ago that it would surely happen ; the
only wonder is it didn't happen before.' Mr.
Tootell, indeed, was frightfully disappointed
that he had not been the first to distribute
such a toothsome piece of scandal. He
blamed himself severely for having been
rather remiss lately in visiting the Dragon ; but
Mr. Johnson, alias Creasey, had so occupied
his attention that he had not found time to
attend to the Mercer family. The *soi-disant*
Johnson was a most tantalising mystery to
him. What that gentleman's business or
pleasure might be down at Exmouth he was
unable to discover. Two singular things in
his conversation were his great curiosity
about the old Dragon Inn, though often as
Tootell had volunteered to take him out to
see it, he had always declined ; the other was

the numerous inquiries he made about the Lydneys. He asked endless questions about the banker's family, about whom there was little to tell. Mr. Lydney, as far as his neighbours knew, had led the uneventful life of a prosperous country banker, and there was no reason to suppose there was any dark spot on the family escutcheon. One thing Mr. Tootell felt was imperative—to wit, that he must visit the Dragon without loss of time.

'Yes,' he said to one of his intimate cronies, 'I told old Joe how it would be. I warned him, but he paid no attention to me.' The shameless old liar had never ventured to say a word upon the subject. '"A strong-willed gal, Joe," I said, "yes, I grant you that, but you're wrong. It don't do to give 'em their head altogether, even if they do chafe a bit at the curb." I spoke to Sarah

myself about it, too.   Says I, " You're
wasting your time, Sarah "—if he had made
this observation to Miss Mercer his ears would
probably have sung for the next two hours—
" those soldier officers are all gilt and sugar.
You pick up with a good middle-aged trades-
man—that's the man for your money " '—and
here Mr. Tootell paused, almost aghast at his
own mendacity.   ' Well, well,' he continued,
' poor Joe! he's an old pal of mine.   It'll ease
his heart, poor old chap, to tell all his troubles
to me.   I'll go over to-morrow morning and
hear all about it; it'll comfort him, you
know.'

' Yes,' replied his crony, dryly.   ' I should
think, Tootell, you would be a real comfort
to any family in a state of domestic affliction.'

' I am, I am,' returned Tootell, earnestly.
' We should all endeavour to soothe our fellow-

creatures in their hour of anguish. I'll be out there the first thing to-morrow morning, have a pint of mild ale with Joe, and tell him to keep his pecker up. Let you know all about it when I come back. By the way, you don't know a party of the name of Johnson, do you? Here he comes. Can't make out what he's doing here. By-bye ; I must go and talk to him.' And Mr. Tootell trotted off to endeavour once again to turn the reticent Johnson inside out.

The fact that Sarah Mercer had left her home being established beyond question, no one in Exmouth seemed to doubt that Fred Hallaton was the companion of her flight ; and when the news reached Mary Lydney, as it speedily did, she had no little difficulty in maintaining her outward composure. Her father brought the story home with him, and made much lamentation over Fred Hallaton.

'Great pity, great pity,' he said ; 'as nice a young fellow as ever I met; and if this be true—and I've no doubt it is—he has hung a pretty millstone round his neck. I wonder how my old friend Sir Robert will take it ! There's a deal of the General commanding about him, and I'm afraid he'll swear like that army of Flanders at such an infraction of discipline as he will consider this.'

Here Mr. Lydney fell into deep thought, and Mary took advantage of the circumstance to escape from the room. 'Yes,' mused the banker, ' a man's relations generally join in a chorus of loud-tongued abuse when he commits a mistake in life of this sort, and Sir Robert is not the uncle to omit that ceremony. I suppose his best way out of the scrape will be to marry the girl. By-the-by, I wonder what old Joe Mercer will do with his money. Judging from the sums he keeps passing through our bank, he must be making a lot somehow or other. He doesn't keep a very big drawing account, but he has always had the credit of being a warm man, and this year he's had the handling of hundreds, at all events. There's only this girl and her brother, a very wide-awake gentleman, I am told, who has taken to racing as a profession. I don't know anything about the turf myself, but I've always understood gentlemen lose fortunes and bookmakers make them. Poor young Hallaton is not the first man by a good many who has ruined his life for a woman,' and with this the banker dismissed the subject from his thoughts.

When Mary Lydney gained her room she

sat down and gave way to a burst of bitter weeping. Tears principally of shame and anger. She was ashamed to think that for the second time she had allowed her heart to go out of her own keeping, and her pride was cruelly wounded to find what a mockery this love was that Hallaton had professed for her. Not three days after she had scornfully accused him of preferring another woman to herself, he had run off with that very woman. Emotional people are by no means those in whom the passions run deepest, and Mary Lydney, under a placid exterior, concealed a strong, passionate, sensitive nature. Sarah Mercer, wounded in her pride, vanity, or caprice, would have given vent to a storm of angry railing at the delinquent. Mary Lydney would never have opened her lips to a soul. With the first, it would be a skin-deep scratch, and forgotten in twenty-four hours. With the second, the wound would rankle deeply and take long to heal.

Sarah Mercer's elopement, indeed, made no little stir about the county generally. That it should speedily find its way into the local papers was matter of course. Gay, good-looking, a proficient at all games and pastimes, Fred Hallaton had made himself amazingly popular for many miles round Exeter. In country quarters it is usually the fault of the soldiers themselves if they are not constant and welcome guests in all the best houses around, and Fred Hallaton had usually more invitations to dine, sleep, and spend a few days in country houses than, having regard to his military duties, he could possibly accept. Miss Lydney, too, was popular in the county. Her intimates said

there was a good deal of quiet fun in Mary
Lydney when you knew her; so that, take
it all round, Hallaton's escapade was quite
a nine days' wonder. But Exmouth was
destined to be speedily provided with another
sensation.

Mr. Lydney was a magistrate of the
borough, and one morning at breakfast his
servant informed him that a Mrs. McIntosh
wanted to see him.

'Show her into my room,' replied the
banker, 'and say I'll be there in a few minutes.'
And when he had finished his breakfast
Mr. Lydney rose and walked off to see what
Mrs. McIntosh wanted.

'Pray sit down, my good woman,' said the
banker, as he entered the study; 'and then
tell me what I can do for you. It's some
magistrates' business, I suppose.'

'Yes, please sir. It's Mr. Tootell, which he've lodged with me now for four years come last Michaelmas. I've come to you to ask your advice about him.'

'You must be a little more explicit, if you please, Mrs. McIntosh. Mr. Tootell I believe to be a most respectable man. I trust you have no complaint to bring against him.'

'No, poor dear! It's himself I'm frightened about. He's a good, harmless old gentleman, as wouldn't hurt a fly. He gives no trouble; is as quiet, reg'lar lodger as a lone woman need wish to have, only he must know all that goes on in the house. But, deary me, we've all our little failin's, haven't we, sir?'

'Indeed, we have,' thought Mr. Lydney, 'and loquacity is yours, my good woman. Mrs. McIntosh,' he continued aloud, 'I must

ask you to come to the point. I am pressed
for time this morning.'

'Well, sir, Mr. Tootell—an' a more reg'lar
gentleman no widder woman need wish to
meet with—he went out and he never came
home to his dinner.'

'Come, Mrs. McIntosh,' said the banker,
'you really must get on a little quicker than
this. There is nothing remarkable in that.'

'But he never came home to bed, which
he's not done sich a thing ever since he first
came to me.'

'Still, what is it you are wanting?' asked
the banker, impatiently.

'And he didn't come home last night
either, and he've said nothink to me about it,
and nobody has seen him, and I don't know
what to do about it, and I thought p'raps
some of you gentlemen would make inquiries.

He ought to be looked for, sir, oughtn't he? He ought to be found, and not to be allowed to go rampaging about without notice like this, frightening a poor woman out of her senses.'

'That's all you've to say, then?' observed Mr. Lydney.

'All,' replied Mrs. McIntosh.

The banker hastened to stop the flood of useless information with which he saw the applicant was about to overwhelm him.

'That will do,' he said. 'I'll attend to the business at once, and direct the police to make all proper inquiries. Then, Mrs. McIntosh, we shall be anxious to hear all you can tell us. Good morning!' and with this Mr. Lydney promptly rang the bell, and his visitor was shown out.

Mr. Tootell was such a prominent figure

about Exmouth that his disappearance would
have been certain to attract considerable
attention, even had not the shrill-tongued
inquiries of Mrs. McIntosh called notice to it.
An inquisitive man with no business of his
own to attend to, and who therefore interested
himself most exasperatingly in the affairs of
his neighbours, he was a well-known character,
and literally pervaded the town. Since he
had given up the White Hart, he had never
been known to go away from Exmouth, and,
indeed, previous to that his absences from
home had been few and far between. When
the banker went out he found that the
mysterious disappearance of Mr. Tootell was
quite the talk of the day; he was compelled
to acknowledge that Mrs. McIntosh had
some reason for wishing inquiries set afoot.
For an elderly gentleman of peculiarly regu-

lar habits to absent himself for a couple of nights without mentioning his intention to any one was undoubtedly a singular circumstance. He had been seen to leave his lodgings in Rolle Street on the Tuesday morning, which was the day after the news of Sarah Mercer's elopement became public property in Exmouth, and since that nobody had set eyes upon him. Late on Wednesday night an acquaintance of Tootell's presented himself at the police station and told them that on the Monday afternoon the missing man had expressed his intention of walking out the next morning to call upon his old friend Mercer at the Dragon Inn.

After the manner of most important witnesses he had been slow to hear of the mystery to the unravelling of which his testimony was probably the clue.

CHAPTER XV

THE MERCERS LEVANT

EARLY the next morning the police went out
to the Dragon to make inquiries for the
missing man, and when the constable came
back his news made Mr. Tootell's disappearance more mysterious than ever. He reported
that he found the Dragon shut up; all the
lower windows were closed and bolted, and
there was not the slightest sign of any one
being on the premises. He had knocked
loudly at the door, but his knocking had met
with no response; he had been round the
house, but could see no means of effecting
an entry except by force. He had met one

of the maid-servants who had been employed at the house, who told him that she and the other girl had been paid their full wages to the end of the quarter the previous night, and at the same time they were informed that their services would be no longer required, as the Dragon was such a losing concern that Mr. Mercer meant to close it at once; perhaps the young lady who had charge of the bar could tell more about it. The police speedily called upon her—but no; her experience was exactly the same as that of the two maid-servants. She also had been settled with in similar fashion, and told she would be no longer required, the attempt to reopen the old inn having been a miserable failure. Asked if she knew Mr. Tootell by sight, she laughed and said, 'Certainly!'— that he was a constant visitor at the Dragon.

On further inquiry as to when she saw him last, she replied unhesitatingly, 'On Tuesday.' That he had called, after his usual custom in the morning, and she had taken him a pint of ale into the bar parlour. She did not see him leave the house, but it was quite possible that he might have done so without her noticing it. The bar-parlour was a room at the back of the bar, but not connected with it.

When these facts were reported to Mr. Lydney he proceeded to confer with one of his brother magistrates. Joe Mercer was a man passing honest; that the Dragon had turned out a losing concern was simply what every one had predicted; he seemed to have paid all his servants, and had, as Mr. Lydney well knew, a drawing account in his hands— somewhat smaller, it is true, than he usually

kept there, but still there was nothing to
warrant any suspicion that Joe Mercer was
running away from his creditors. That
Mercer had a perfect right to lock up his
house and close a losing concern nobody could
deny ; and the magistrates debated for some
time whether they were justified in ordering
the police to break into the Dragon. That
Tootell and Mercer were friends of long
standing there were plenty of people to bear
witness to ; neither of them was a violent-
tempered man, nor was there the slightest
suspicion of there being any ill-blood between
them ; but yet Mr. Tootell, contrary to all
his usual habits, had disappeared suddenly
and mysteriously, and the last place in which
he had been seen was in the bar-parlour
of the Dragon. The magistrates hesitated.
Were the circumstances such as justified

them in breaking into Joe Mercer's locked-
up house? Mr. Lydney recalled to mind the
famous skating accident of some years ago
in the Regent's Park, and remembered how
many people who started with the avowed
intention of spending their afternoon on the
ice, and who were supposed to have been
drowned, had turned up afterwards, having
changed their minds suddenly and left
London on the spur of the moment. Who
should say that Mr. Tootell had not been
seized with a similar hasty impulse, and
accompanied his old friend Mercer on his
unexpected travels? There really did seem
hardly sufficient grounds for supposing that
any harm had befallen Tootell. But the
sudden disappearance of that gentleman and
the elopement of Sarah Mercer had invested
the Dragon with a halo of romance, and

people began to recall some of the half-forgotten stories connected with the inn. Many of the idlers of the town flocked out to look at it, and, amongst others, 'the party of the name of Johnson.' Very soon a message came back to Exmouth to say that there was somebody in the house, and the excitement of the people outside rose to fever heat; the police, and with them Mr. Lydney and one of his brother magistrates, were soon upon the scene, and after a short time there could be distinctly heard a faint cry of ' Hi ! Halloa ! Help, somebody !'

The magistrates at once gave orders to break open the door ; but this turned out to be a more troublesome business than was anticipated, the front door of the inn being a good solid portal of tough oak, and lavishly furnished with bolts and bars. Suddenly one of the more enterprising of the spectators, who had gone round to the back of the house, said that the cries for help distinctly came from the leg of the building that ran into the garden, and that it would be easier to force an entrance through one of the windows there than to break in at the door. · An attack was accordingly made upon one of the windows of the old ball-room. To smash through one of the windows was simple enough, but they had been boarded up from within with considerable solidity. Still, a very few minutes sufficed to make a breach in it, and as soon as the opening was large enough one of the constables entered, but at first, in the darkness of the room, could see nothing. He called to those at work outside to enlarge the opening, and as he did so, from a far corner of the room came a cry of 'Hi! Help, for God's sake!' The constable, whose eyes were now becoming accustomed to the gloom, made his way cautiously across, and in another minute was bending over the form of the prostrate Tootell, who lay bound hand and foot.

'I have found Mr. Tootell,' he shouted. 'Let in some more light. You're all right, sir, ain't you?'

'Cut these horrible cords,' gasped the luckless man, as the constable raised him. 'I don't know; I'm not sure. I've been shamefully treated.'

By this time the room was full of people, and the boardings of the windows were being rapidly torn down; but so numbed was Mr. Tootell that after his bonds were severed he was at first unable to stand. The police now

took charge of the premises, and quickly
cleared the room of all but themselves, the
magistrates, and the victim, who was at
present too exhausted to give an account of
his mishap, and requested a little stimulant
to restore him to himself.

In pursuit of this the police essayed to
open the door of the ball-room, and being,
like the doors of all old-fashioned houses, sub-
stantially built, it took some time to force.

Those who had obtained an entrance into
the old ball-room had stared round them in
undisguised astonishment; that such a room
existed at the back of the Dragon was a
surprise to most of them. They looked
curiously at the pile of quaint, old-fashioned
furniture which had been heaped together
promiscuously—old-fashioned chairs, tables,
pier-glasses, &c.; superfluities which had

been drawn together from every room in the house. Some were dilapidated, some were serviceable, but all bore the signs of having been good in their day.

However, the police gave little time to look at all these things, for, in spite of the strenuous objections of the curious, they insisted upon clearing the room. One of those who begged most earnestly to be allowed to remain was Mr. Johnson. He asserted that he was an intimate friend of Tootell's, and should be uncomfortable until he had witnessed the complete restoration of that gentleman ; but the police were obdurate, and he, like others, was compelled to retire. Had anybody been watching Mr. Johnson closely it would certainly have struck him that he was more curious about the furniture than anxious about Mr. Tootell. He scanned the chairs and tables narrowly, and when the latter had drawers seemed half-inclined to open them. However, as before said, his investigations, if he was really making such, were speedily brought to a close, and by order of the magistrates the police took charge of the house, with orders to exclude all visitors.

When Mr. Tootell had been taken to the bar-parlour, and had had a tolerably stiff dose of spirits-and-water administered to him, several bottles of which were found in the bar, the magistrates requested him to give some account of what had happened, and explain how it was that they had found him in the plight they did.

'It's a long story, gentlemen,' replied Tootell, in all the glory of being the hero of the hour, 'and I couldn't have believed that

an old friend like Joe Mercer could have
behaved so.'

'He is quite right,' whispered Mr.
Lydney to one of his brother magistrates.
'It will be a long story.'

'Well, gentlemen, you all know the misfor-
tune which befell poor old Joe. You know
how his daughter ran away and left him. I'm
not one of that sort who don't stick to my
friends in their trouble; so I thought on
Tuesday morning I'd just walk over and
cheer him up a bit. I'm an observant man,
gentlemen, and I'd noticed usually that when
I came over to the Dragon there was a party
of the name of Brent hanging about—in fact,
he lived here, and I never could make out
what he was doing in this neighbourhood, or
what he had come here for. Now, I always
look upon it as a suspicious circumstance, as

I dare say you do too, gentlemen, that a man
should be loafing about a place for no particular reason. At first I thought he had
come after Miss Mercer ; and as I've always
taken a friendly interest in that young woman,
I ventured to hint as much ; and she was that
rude to me that at first I felt convinced my
suspicions were well founded ; but when that
young chap Hallaton came hanging about I
saw I was wrong.'

' Really, Mr. Tootell,' said the banker, ' we
must ask you to come to the point ; all this
has nothing to do with the state in which
we found you. Tell us briefly who you were
assaulted by, and, I suppose I may say,
imprisoned.'

' You must understand the case, sir, in all
its bearings,' replied Tootell, with great solemnity. ' Very few men have gone through such

a wonderful experience in the course of their lives. I shall make you open your eyes, gentlemen, before I've done.'

'He never will!' murmured the banker.

'Well,' continued Tootell, 'Mercer didn't receive my sympathy in the spirit I could have wished. In fact, he murmured something about "inquisitive people," and I'd just made up my mind that he was an ungrateful beast and that I'd bother my head no more about his troubles, when in came this man Brent. Now, you know what an aggravating thing it is, gentlemen, to think you recollect a face, but not to be able to call to mind where you've seen it. This was just my case with Brent. The last time I had been over to the Dragon I felt pretty certain that he wore a wig, and I thought if I saw him without his wig I might perhaps recognise him. He seemed a little disconcerted at seeing me, but there was no doubt about it—he did wear a wig. He had seated himself between me and the door, and when I got up to go shortly afterwards I caught my foot in the carpet, and stumbled up against him to save myself from falling. Somehow or other Mr. Brent's wig got knocked off in the scuffle, and I recognised him.'

'I presume, Mr. Tootell,' said the banker, laughing, 'that this was quite accidental on your part?'

'I don't deny, gentlemen, but what I made the most of the accident. But people that wear wigs, and are doing nobody knows what, ought to be looked after.'

'And what happened then?' inquired one of the magistrates.

'This Brent flew at me like a wild cat. Took me by the throat before I could utter a syllable, and then he and Mercer hustled me into the ball-room. A nice bit of gratitude that, on old Joe's part, to one who's been a friend to him all his life ! '

It would have been rather difficult to say what particular claim Mr. Tootell had on the gratitude of the landlord of the Dragon.

' When they got me in there,' he continued, ' they told me no harm was going to happen to me so long as I held my tongue. Then there was a hurried consultation between them in a low tone, at the end of which that insolent Brent told me that as I chose to poke my nose into things that didn't concern me I must take the consequences ; that no harm would come to me, but as I had persisted in coming where I wasn't wanted, it was now necessary that I should stay there for the next forty-eight hours, and that if I gave no trouble

I should find myself decently treated. You saw, gentlemen, with your own eyes, what the brute's idea of decent treatment was.'

'Then,' said Mr. Lydney, ' you were kept locked up in that old ball-room all the time?'

'Oh, no; indeed I wasn't. There are immense cellars under that old ball-room. They are a sight to see, gentlemen—it'll be necessary you should see them—and I was kept down there till a little before daybreak this morning. Then I was brought upstairs, tied as you found me, informed that people would come and release me in the course of the day, locked in, and left.'

'And what on earth was the reason of this unprovoked assault and imprisonment?'

'Because,' replied Tootell, 'I had recognised Brent, and found out why Joe Mercer took the old Dragon Inn.'

CHAPTER XVI

WHY JOE TOOK THE DRAGON

Now, why Joe Mercer had taken the Dragon had not only puzzled his friends, but set a considerable portion of the people of Exmouth talking. Even the magistrates, when he had applied for a licence, had wondered what on earth the man could want with a house from which the custom had departed years ago, and nearly decided not to grant it, on the grounds that it was not needed by the public. That Mercer's mysterious reasons for embarking in such a hopeless concern were about to be laid bare excited the interest of Mr Lydney and his brother magistrates not a little.

'You say that we shall have to see these cellars, Mr. Tootell, and no doubt we shall; but before we do so I must ask you one question—Under what name did you know this man Brent, and in what capacity did you know him?'

'I knew him before I came to Exmouth. He went then by the name of Jackson, and,' continued Mr. Tootell, with some hesitation, 'I had business relations with him.'

'Of what nature?' asked Mr. Lydney.

'Well, he represented himself as traveller for a distillery.'

'Ah, you had dealings with him?'

'Just so,' replied Mr. Tootell, with a brevity in striking contrast to his usual garrulity.

The retired publican, in truth, was by no means anxious to go into the details of his

former dealings with Brent. He had bought
spirits from that worthy when he kept a
tavern in London. He had carefully abstained
from asking questions, but from the quality
and price of the liquors had always had
misgivings that they were fraudulently come
by.

'Now,' said Mr. Lydney, turning to the
police, 'get a light, some of you, and let us
go and see these cellars. They are under the
ball-room, I think you said?'

'Yes,' replied Tootell; 'there's a trapdoor
in the corner leads down to them.'

Lights were soon procured. The trap-
door was easily lifted, and disclosed a short
flight of stone steps. They descended these,
and found themselves in a moderate-sized
but remarkably dry vaulted room, which bore
signs of recent occupation. There was a

truckle-bed in one corner, a couple of chairs and a table, and a shelf or two, garnished with a few drinking-cups and platters.

'Well,' said the banker, as he looked around him, 'no man ever lived here from choice. Whoever has been occupying this place must have had motives for concealment, and except for his assault upon you there doesn't seem to be anything against Brent.'

However, at the further end of this room were two low archways, each of which led to a vaulted cellar of much larger dimensions than the first, and in both of these inner vaults there were signs in abundance of the occupation of their late inmates.

'Looks as if they had been brewing of something,' said one of the policemen, pointing to the extinguished furnace, which was surmounted by a large, globular-shaped copper vessel surrounded by brickwork.

‘What a very odd place to have a copper!’ said Mr. Lydney. ‘And what a deuced oddly-shaped one!’

‘Don’t you know what it is, sir?’ said Mr. Tootell. ‘Why, that’s a still. You just send into Exmouth for one of the excise officers, and he’ll precious soon let you know all about it.’

‘Go and fetch an excise officer at once,’ said Mr. Lydney, turning to the police. ‘Who would have dreamt of there being such immense vaults in connection with the Dragon as these?’

‘Ah, they must have been built in the old smuggling days,’ rejoined one of his brother magistrates, ‘and no doubt have held many a contraband cargo in their time.’

Although neither Mr. Lydney nor his brethren were conversant with distilling, they had no doubt whatever that Tootell was right. He told them he did not understand the process, but he had seen a distillery in London, and could not be mistaken.

Pending the arrival of the excise officer they adjourned to the bar-parlour once more.

'Let me see,' said Mr. Lydney. 'Mercer took this house at the beginning of the year, and opened it two months afterwards; he must have been carrying on this illegal distillery for close on twelve months.' And then the magistrates amused themselves with trying to calculate what sum Mercer might have made at this nefarious business, and in this speculation they were assisted by the experiences of Mr. Tootell.

When the excise officer arrived they once more adjourned to the cellars.

'Weugh!' exclaimed that worthy, 'this is a proper little game to have been carried on under our noses. To think of old Mercer going in for such a plant as this; why, this is as complete a still as ever I saw. Look here, gentlemen, you see in this cellar to the left they've got their mash-tun, refrigerators, pump in the corner, water laid on, everything; and here, in this cellar to the right, is the still itself, and not a little one either.'

'And how much spirits do you suppose they could make a week?' asked Mr. Lydney.

'Impossible to say, sir; five or six hundred gallons—may be more; but considering the Government duty is ten shillings a gallon, that would be good enough for them; that would mean they would make two or three hundred pounds a week, or a thousand to twelve hundred a month.'

'God bless me!' said one of the magistrates. 'And do you suppose Mercer to have made five or six thousand pounds in this inn?'

'Every bit of it—that is, he and his partners, for there must have been more in it than he and Brent. You see, it takes three or four of them to work a still, gentlemen. During the actual distilling they can't leave the furnace for a minute, and when they are fermenting, as they would be, in the other room, that requires watching almost as close.'

'Well,' said Mr. Lydney, 'I had no idea that taking the Dragon was as good as that; why, this old fox Mercer was doing a better business than any hotel in Exmouth. However, he has fairly slipped us, and I suppose there is nothing to do but to issue warrants against him and Brent, *alias* Jackson, on a charge of defrauding the revenue. By the way, do you know anything about this Brent ? '

' Nothing, sir,' replied the officer, ' but it's very likely they will in London. You see, the men who go in for this style of fraud are a very limited number. It requires a considerable amount of chemical knowledge. Those who have acquired proficiency at it try it on again and again, the profits are so enormous, and the principal hands engaged in it are pretty well known at head-quarters.'

' Well,' said Mr. Lydney, turning to the chief constable, ' you had better fasten up the house again, barricade the windows we've broken open, and then, as soon as we can get back to the town, we'll have those warrants made out for you.'

Mr. Tootell was more than repaid for past suffering on his return to Exmouth. He was the hero of the hour, and people crowded round him to hear the story from his own lips. The news that he had been found had reached the town some time before, accompanied by a somewhat indefinite rumour of extraordinary revelations at the old Dragon Inn. A skeleton had been found there; the proceeds of long-forgotten robberies had been discovered in the cellars; the mystery of a murder which had taken place many years ago had been solved; in short, there was no end to the wild rumours about the discoveries made in the search for Tootell; local reporters who had vainly sought to be admitted now thronged round the rescued

man to learn all particulars. The *Exmouth
Gazette* was full of it the next morning, and
a day later the London papers—it was the
dead season—contained paragraphs headed—
'Singular discovery of an illicit still in Devonshire.' If Mr. Tootell was the lion of the
day no one could complain that he refused
to roar. His good-nature in relating his adventures knew no bounds, and the wonderful
manner in which his moving tale amplified
by continued narration was a source of infinite mirth to some of the wags of Exmouth.
One of these latter, indeed, observed that it
was impossible to picture any bounds to
Tootell's adventures. ' I think,' observed this
young humourist, ' it was about the eighth
time I had induced him to tell me his story,
and he never was more brilliant. His following the conspirators down the cellar-steps,

determined to discover what their desperate
calling might be, his frightful struggle with
four reckless smugglers by the side of the
still, was most melodramatic and artistic.
Give old Tootell time, and he'll work up
that adventure of his into a thrilling romance.
It'll become something blood-curdling before
he dies, see if it won't.'

The London authorities on being communicated with replied that it was of course
impossible for them to say for certain, but
they should judge it to be the work of a man
called Jackson, if that was indeed his real
name, for his *aliases* had been innumerable.
'He is the most daring and successful modern
smuggler of our times. Illicit distillation is
this man's favourite game, and though we
have never as yet been able to lay hands on
him, this, if it be he, is only one of a life-

long series of frauds on the revenue. He does not confine himself entirely to this line of fraud, but, curiously enough, his enterprises always partake of this nature, insomuch that they are usually frauds upon the revenue in some shape. He was originally a clerk in a large London distillery, in the working of which he took the greatest interest, and of course it was there he acquired his proficiency in the process. After two or three years he got into money difficulties and absconded. His books were examined, showing a considerable deficit to his employers. Since that he has turned up pretty regularly every three or four years, engaged in some such illegal business under a different name. He has led this life since quite a young man, for he was only about four or five and twenty when he first came under our notice. It is not of

much use describing him, for we have no
description of him upon which we can rely,
although we have half a dozen which profess
to depict him ; but one of the man's pecu-
liarities is that when he embarks on one of
his frauds he invariably disguises himself
with considerable cleverness, and the consequence is that " Slippery Bill's " personality
is hardly known to his confederates.'

When Mr. Lydney read the account of
the London police he remarked to his
brethren on the Bench, 'There can be little
doubt, I think, that Brent is the man. He
evidently attaches great importance to con-
cealing his identity, and when Tootell,
maddened by curiosity, knocked off his wig
—well, he suppressed Tootell till he had
achieved his escape.'

The morning after Tootell's rescue Mr.

Lydney had been somewhat astonished by the advent of a visitor who sent in a request to speak to him. The banker ordered him to be shown into his study, and upon entering it a man in the garb of a farm labourer said—

'Well, measter, I was told to give 'ee this, and this bit of a note.' And the man handed the banker a heavy key and the letter.

'What is this the key of?' inquired Mr. Lydney.

'I dunno for sure,' was the reply, 'but I reckon it'll fit the side door of the Dragon.'

'And who gave it to you?'

'Muster Mercer.'

'Ah! where did you leave him?'

'I druv him, the missis, and that 'ere Brent chap to Exeter before daybreak yesterday morning.'

'What, to the station?' asked Mr. Lydney.

'Yes; and he told me I was to bait my horse, and when I got up hoame I was to bring that 'ere key and note to you.'

'And why didn't you do it?' inquired the banker, sharply.

'Well, I got hoame so late,' replied the man, rather sheepishly.

'Let me see,' said the banker, 'you reached Exeter about eight o'clock, and, allowing for getting your breakfast and baiting your horse, ought to have been back again at the Dragon a little after midday at the latest. Come, tell me the truth about this. I suppose the fact is you got drunk?'

'Well, and that's a fact, measter,' replied the man. 'Muster Mercer and Muster Brent were both that liberal to me on going away I

got a drop too much, and then I fell among
a lot of chaps as were good company, and I
got a drop more, and then I fell asleep like.'

'That'll do,' replied the banker, 'you
may go now. Lucky for my friend Tootell
we discovered him, or he would have been
locked up in the Dragon still. What an
appetite he'd have had for breakfast!' And
then Mr. Lydney bethought himself of the
note which he was still twisting between his
fingers, and opened it.

'The bearer of this will give you the key
of the side door of the Dragon Inn. You
had better send out at once, as you will find
Tootell locked up in the old ball-room.
He owes his disagreeable position to his
unfortunate propensity for poking his nose
into other people's affairs. I feel quite sure
that any inconvenience he may have suffered

will be amply compensated for by the gratification of his curiosity.—J. MERCER.'

'Ah!' said the banker, musingly, 'Joe Mercer never wrote that. To begin with, it's the letter of a much better educated man than he is; and, secondly, I am his banker, and therefore perfectly acquainted with Joe Mercer's signature and handwriting. Now, if he didn't write it, it must have been Brent who did. I will take care of this, it might come in useful some day.' And with that the banker carefully locked up the note in his escritoire.

END OF THE FIRST VOLUME.

Spottiswoode & Co. Printers, New-street Square, London

www.ingramcontent.com/pod-product-compliance
Lightning Source LLC
Chambersburg PA
CBHW020852020726
47497CB00005B/1377